The Election Calculation

Book 10 in **The Math Kids** Series

The Math Kids Series
Have you read them all?

1. The Prime-Time Burglars
2. A Sequence of Events
3. An Unusual Pattern
4. An Encrypted Clue
5. An Incorrect Solution
6. The Triangle Secret
7. A Knotty Problem
8. An Artificial Test
9. An Unsolved Proof

The Election Calculation

Book 10 in **The Math Kids** Series

by
David Cole

Common Deer Press

Published by Common Deer Press Incorporated

Text Copyright © 2024 David Cole
Illustration Copyright © Shannon O'Toole

All rights reserved under International and Pan-American Copyright conventions. No part of this book may be reproduced in any form or by any electronic or mechanical means, including information storage and retrieval systems, without permission in writing from the publisher, except by a reviewer, who may quote brief passages in a review.

Published in 2024 by Common Deer Press
1745 Rockland Avenue
Victoria, British Columbia
V8S 1W6

This book is a work of fiction. Names, characters, places, and incidents are either the product of the author's imagination or are used fictitiously.

Library and Archives Canada Cataloguing in Publication

Title: The election calculation / by David Cole.
Names: Cole, David, 1957- author.
Series: Cole, David, 1957- Math kids ; bk. 10.
Description: Series statement: The math kids series ; book 10
Identifiers: Canadiana (print) 20230582508 | Canadiana (ebook) 20230582516 | ISBN 9781988761985 (softcover) | ISBN 9781988761992 (EPUB)
Subjects: LCGFT: Novels.
Classification: LCC PZ7.1.C64 Ele 2024 | DDC j813/.6—dc23

Cover Image: Shannon O'Toole
Book Design: David Moratto

Printed in Canada
www.CommonDeerPress.com

To all the parent volunteers who coach sports teams, read to children, assist on field trips, help kids to improve their academics, or in whatever capacity you are serving—thank you!

Chapter 1

Catherine Duchesne took a deep breath as she stood on the sidewalk in front of Tyler Middle School. It was easily three times the size of McNair Elementary, where she had gone since kindergarten.

"You ready for this?" came a voice from behind her. Catherine jumped and quickly turned around to see Stephanie Lewis, her best friend.

"I guess," Catherine replied with a little uncertainty in her voice.

"It's going to be weird being in different classes," Stephanie said.

Rather than having the same teacher all day as they had had at McNair, they would now be switching between different classes for each subject. The two girls had gotten their schedules mailed to them over the weekend and had quickly compared them. They were disappointed to learn they would only have two classes in common when school started in a couple of weeks.

"Well, at least we'll be in math class together," Catherine said.

"Yeah, I checked with the guys and they're also in that class," Stephanie said, "so the Math Kids will still see each other every day."

The Math Kids was a club that Stephanie, Jordan Waters, and Justin Grant had formed in fourth grade. The original intent was to solve math puzzles, but they had also used their math skills to solve real world problems like robberies. Working as a team, they'd even assisted the FBI and Scotland Yard.

"Speaking of the guys, there they are," Catherine said, pointing to a car pulling up to the curb in front of the school.

Jordan and Justin hopped out of the car and joined Catherine and Stephanie on the sidewalk.

"I guess this is going to be our home for the next three years," Jordan said.

"I guess," Catherine said.

"That didn't sound very positive," Justin said. "Personally, I can't wait. You know they have a math team, don't you? They went to the state championship last year. They didn't win, but then again, they didn't have us."

"What if we're not good enough to make the team?" Catherine asked.

"Not make the team?" Justin asked incredulously. "They'll be begging us to be on the team once they see what we can do!"

The Election Calculation

"I hope so," Jordan said. "Linda said they have lots of other clubs too. She said everyone has to join at least two clubs in sixth grade." He said this with a touch of doubt. His sister Linda was a few years older than him and loved to tease her younger brother, so he didn't always believe everything she said.

"I heard they have a gaming club!" Justin said. "I bet they have all the coolest new video games and consoles." If there was anything Justin liked almost as much as math, it was playing video games.

"Do you think they have a robotics club?" Catherine asked. "I loved the robotics camp I did this summer."

"That's why we're here," Jordan said. He pointed at a sign near the entrance that read *Club Exhibition: Come find a club that's just right for you!*

"Then I guess we should go in and see what they have," Catherine said.

They entered the school and followed signs leading them to the gymnasium. Inside, they found dozens of tables where students were answering questions about their club.

"Wow! Look at this!" Stephanie exclaimed. "Judo club. Cooking club. Anime club. It looks like they've got something for everyone."

Justin spotted a large video screen that had a car careening left and right across a road while the driver tried to avoid falling boulders. "I think I found my people," he said as he walked quickly in that direction.

"You're not going with him?" Catherine asked Jordan.

"Nah, I'll never be as good as him in video games. I'm going to look around to see what else I can find."

"I'm going to see if they have a soccer club," Stephanie said. She headed toward the far wall, scanning the club names as she went.

That left Catherine all by herself. She walked slowly in the opposite direction. She took her time reading a brief description of each club and sometimes engaging one of the club members to learn more. The robotics club looked very interesting. Their table display showed several completed robots they had made the previous year. One of them was designed to solve a Rubik's Cube puzzle and Catherine spent a few minutes scrambling the Cube and watching the robot undo her moves.

The photography club had a book of pictures the members had taken over the past several years. She didn't know much about photography, but she pored over landscapes, action shots of athletes taken with a telephoto lens, and a really cool close-up of a spider spinning a web.

"I took that one," a girl in a brightly colored t-shirt said. "I used a macro lens at f/2.8 and a shutter speed of 1/125th of a second."

Catherine didn't know what any of that meant, which intrigued her. She took a handout for the club so she could read more about it later.

The Election Calculation

There were clubs for all kinds of games—board games, card games, role-playing games, chess, checkers, and several games Catherine had never heard of. There were half a dozen music clubs, both singing and playing instruments, and one whose description said, "We just hang out and listen to music."

A lot of the clubs looked interesting, and Catherine was gathering a stack of handouts for clubs she might want to check out further. As she rounded the corner to walk down the final row of tables, she saw a tall thin boy with round glasses sitting alone at one of the tables. The sign on the table said *Geocaching: The world's biggest treasure hunt.* Catherine was immediately intrigued.

"What's geocaching?" she asked the boy.

"It's a kind of treasure hunt where you look for hidden caches of objects," he replied. "You can think of it as a hide-and-seek game. The hiders provide online clues for the seekers. The seekers—that's us—use global positioning system devices to find the hidden caches."

"And you can do that around here?"

"You bet!" he said, his voice rising a little in his excitement. "I've now found more than forty caches, and I've only been doing it for a year."

As he described the process for seeking out a cache, Catherine found herself getting hooked on the idea of hunting for hidden treasure.

"It's not like you're going to find gold or anything," he said.

"Been there, done that," Catherine responded, thinking back to the treasure in gold she and her friends had found in a dark tunnel under the old Maynard mansion.

The boy gave her a strange look but continued. "Once you find the cache, you write your name and the date in the logbook, so they know you were there. Then you take some swag and leave some of your own."

"What's swag?" Catherine asked.

The boy laughed. "It stands for 'stuff we all get,'" he said. "Here's some of the stuff I got over the past year."

He opened the lid on a plastic container and proudly displayed his collection of swag. Catherine smiled broadly when she saw what he had amassed.

"How many people are in the club?" she asked.

"Just me so far," he admitted, his face turning a bright red. "But I hope I can get some people to join me."

"Well, I think maybe your club just doubled in size," Catherine said. "It sounds like fun."

With her mind made up on her second club selection, it was time to find the rest of her friends so they could go check out the math club. She found Stephanie in a discussion with a group of girls at the student newspaper table. Jordan joined them a few minutes later. After a few attempts, the three were able to drag Justin away from the gaming club table, where he was engaged with another boy in battle for bragging rights in an auto race game.

The Election Calculation

"You just barely beat me," Justin called back to the boy. "I'll be back."

The boy gave a half-hearted wave and returned to playing the game.

"I was right," Justin said excitedly, "they do have all the latest games. That's definitely my club pick."

"Did you even look at any of the other clubs?" Jordan asked.

"Well, no, but why bother?"

Jordan shook his head. "But now on to the real reason we're here. Where's the math club?"

"Over in that corner," Stephanie replied, pointing to a table near a rolling cart filled with basketballs.

The four friends were walking toward the table when Justin abruptly stopped in his tracks. Catherine, unable to stop, ran into him.

"What's up with you?" Catherine asked. "Why'd you stop?"

"Look who's at the table," Justin replied.

Catherine looked and immediately understood why her friend had stopped.

Just a month earlier, Justin had been accused of stealing comic books from a store in the mall. Sitting behind the math club table were the two boys who had really stolen the comics and framed him.

Buzz Aquino, the bigger of the two boys, looked up

from the table and recognized Justin and his friends. He elbowed Kenny Hanley in the side.

"Ow! What was that for?" Kenny asked.

"It's those kids from the mall," Buzz answered.

Kenny's face reddened and he clenched his fists.

"Hey, loser," he called out to Justin. "You and your friends got us kicked out of the mall."

"You got yourself kicked out when you stole those comics," Stephanie responded firmly.

"Oh yeah?" Buzz shot back. "It never would have happened if you had just minded your own business. We ought to pound you into the ground."

Buzz took a step forward but stopped when Kenny grabbed his arm. He whispered a few words into his ear and Buzz smirked.

"There's a rumor going around that you four are pretty good at math," Kenny said.

"That's not a rumor," Stephanie said defiantly. "It's a fact."

"That's too bad. You see, we have a *really* good math team," Buzz said. "I'm not so sure that *pretty good* quite meets our standards for making the team."

"And who are you to make that call?" Catherine asked.

"As it so happens, I'm the president of the math club," Kenny said with a cool grin. "And as president, one of my duties is to make the final choice on who competes for the team."

"That's not fair!" Catherine cried out in frustration.

"Nobody said life was fair," Kenny said with a shrug of his shoulders. "It looks like your math competition days are over, at least as long as I'm in charge."

As Kenny turned away, Justin whispered to his friends. "It looks like we have to find a way to elect a new president."

Chapter 2

The start of middle school was like being sent to a foreign country without knowing the language or the customs of the people. Everything was so different from elementary school. The building was huge. There were lots more rooms, lots more teachers, and lots more kids. Jordan got lost at least a dozen times in the first week.

"You're late again," his Beginning Spanish teacher told him as he tried to sneak into the room five minutes after the start of class. Señor Hernandez pointed at the clock. "¿Sabes que hora es?"

Jordan stared at him blankly, not having any idea what his teacher had just said. It sounded like a question, and probably had something to do with time, but other than that he had no clue. The class snickered at his discomfort.

"Maybe if you'd start showing up on time, you'd know I just asked you what time it is," the teacher said, prompting more laughter from the class.

"Yes, sir. Um i-i-," Jordan stammered. "I mean, it's nine o five."

"En español por favor," his teacher prompted.

"Um," Jordan started. He counted on his fingers, trying to remember the Spanish numbers he had been working to memorize. "Um, nueve y cinco?"

The teacher nodded and pointed Jordan toward his seat. "Next time, let's try getting here at nueve, okay?"

***

Things weren't going any better for Justin. He was used to being one of the shortest kids in his class, but now walking in the hallway felt like he was hiking in a forest of legs. It seemed like everyone was at least a head taller than him.

"Sorry, didn't see you there," said a huge kid in blue jeans and a t-shirt who had bumped into him as he passed. Justin just nodded and tried to make it through a horde of people to get to his locker.

"Out of the way, shorty!"

He was pushed aside as a boy rushed past him. Justin gave up and decided he would just carry all his books with him rather than fight his way to his locker every day. It would mean he would have to empty his backpack of his "important stuff" to fit in all the books. The two decks of cards, one blue-backed with only fifty-one cards and a red-backed deck with forty-nine, would have to be left

The Election Calculation

behind, along with a ball of rubber bands, a short length of rope, six batteries of assorted sizes (some with no charge left), his Rubik's Cube, a pair of sunglasses missing one lens, a calculator with a cracked screen, and assorted pens, pencils, and markers. He'd keep his trusty notebook and two sharpened pencils, but everything else would have to go.

The bell rang, meaning he was probably going to be late again. He heaved a sigh and trudged through the crowd toward his social studies class.

***

Catherine passed Stephanie in the hallway but only had time to wave a hand before hurrying on her way to the office. She only had a few minutes between classes and needed to talk to the principal.

"What can I do for you, young lady?" the school secretary asked as she looked at Catherine over the top of her glasses.

"I need to talk with someone about rearranging my classes," she answered. "You see, there's no way that—"

"You'll need to see your guidance counselor," the secretary interrupted.

"I did, but—"

"Are you a sixth grader?" she interrupted again.

"Yes, ma'am."

"Then you'll want to see Mrs. Ramsey."

Catherine started to say something, but the secretary was tapping on her laptop again. Catherine sighed deeply. Middle school was so different. At McNair Elementary, the school secretary always had time for her. She didn't have to go through a list of people to find the right one to help her.

"You're going to be late for class," the secretary said without looking up.

***

Stephanie made it to her biology class with a minute to spare. She was a little nervous because they were supposed to pair up for their first team project. She wasn't concerned about the project—dissecting a frog—but finding someone who would be her partner had her nervously tugging on her ponytail. Most of the kids seemed to know each other, but she didn't know a single person. What if no one wanted to be her partner? She didn't know why she was suddenly worried about this. When she had been the new kid in the class in fourth grade, she just marched in like she owned the place. Why was middle school so different?

"Okay, class, let's talk about dissection," Ms. Bainbridge said as everyone settled onto their stools arranged around lab tables.

"Let's start slicing and dicing," one of the boys said. His buddies at his lab table laughed.

The Election Calculation

Miss Bainbridge frowned. "Dissection is not 'slicing and dicing.' While the animals we'll be dissecting this semester are dead, they are for educational purposes and should always be treated with respect."

The boy turned red and looked down to avoid her serious expression.

"Also, and this is very important," Miss Bainbridge continued, "we'll be using scissors, scalpels, and pins during the dissection. These are all very sharp and I don't want to see anyone get hurt. That means always using care when cutting. In other words, no 'slicing and dicing,' Phil." The class laughed. "Okay, let's divide up into partners."

This was the part Stephanie had been dreading. Two by two, the class quickly paired up, but no one approached her. She looked around for someone who looked like they needed a partner, but there didn't seem to be anyone who wasn't already matched up with someone.

"Can't find a partner?" Miss Bainbridge asked.

"Um, it looks like we have an odd number of people," Stephanie said.

"Okay, how about you join this group of two up here in the front."

She walked over to the lab table where two girls were talking animatedly.

"Hi, I'm Stephanie," she said. "I guess I'm going to be joining your group."

The two girls looked at her, but neither introduced themselves. Stephanie sighed. It's going to be a long year.

***

Lunch and math class were the only times the four Math Kids were all together. It was nice to see some friendly faces in the cafeteria.

"I don't think I'm going to like middle school," Justin said. He was picking at his lunch, taking a few occasional nibbles from his ham and cheese sandwich.

"Me either," Jordan said, who obviously wasn't letting it affect his appetite. Around a mouthful of peanut butter sandwich, he continued, "This school is like a maze. I still can't find any of my classrooms. I sat through ten minutes of eighth grade chemistry this morning because I went to the wrong room."

"Did you learn anything?" Catherine asked.

"Didn't understand a word the teacher said," Jordan admitted. "I hope that's not a required class."

"I think it is."

Jordan looked around the room. "Well, I guess I'd better get used to this place, then. If I have to pass eighth grade chemistry, I'll probably be here for a long time. On the bright side, maybe I'll finally figure out how to get from the gym to my Spanish class."

"Well, I've figured out that there is no way to get from the gym to social studies in five minutes," Catherine said. "I've tried three different routes, but I'm still late every class."

The Election Calculation

"Why don't you talk to your counselor about switching your classes around?" Stephanie asked.

"I tried, but it looks like I'm stuck, at least for now."

"Do you at least like your classes?" Stephanie asked.

"They're okay, I guess, but I don't know how well I'll do," Catherine answered. "There is an awful lot of homework in middle school."

"At least we'll all do well in math," Stephanie said, "so we've got that going for us."

"Maybe," Catherine said. "And speaking of math, I ran into Josh Benson at lunch yesterday."

Josh was on the Armstrong Elementary team they had beat in the district finals in the spring.

"Is he going to be at math club today?" Stephanie asked.

"He said he was," Catherine said.

"Great," Stephanie said. "It will be nice to have at least one friendly face there."

"Yeah, if President Kenny will allow us to go," Jordan said.

"I think all the clubs are open," Catherine said. "I don't think he can keep us out."

"Maybe not, but he can sure stop us from competing."

"You don't think he was just saying that do you?" Stephanie asked anxiously.

"No, I don't," Justin replied. "I think he'll do anything he can to keep us out of the competition."

"Then we have to find a way to change his mind," Jordan said.

Chapter 3

The following Tuesday, Stephanie attended her first meeting for the school newspaper. She looked around and saw the group was an even mix of boys and girls. Mrs. Bronson, her English teacher, headed up the club.

"Let's get started, shall we?" she said from the front of the room. Everyone settled into their seats and looked up at her.

"It's good to see some new faces," she said. "And some familiar faces, of course. I think we're going to have a great year. I'm happy to announce that Dylan Bridgers and Marissa Marshall will be our co-editors of *Tyler Talk* this year. Both were assistant editors last year, so they should know their way around by now."

Dylan and Marissa half-rose from their chairs and acknowledged the scattered applause from the other kids in the room. Dylan was a tall, gangly looking eighth grader with light brown hair. Marissa was also in eighth

The Election Calculation

grade and was very pretty, with long blonde hair pulled back into a ponytail. She smiled and blushed at the attention.

"We put out a paper every other Friday," Mrs. Bronson continued. "It's a lot of work and the only way we can meet those deadlines is if everyone contributes. We need all kinds of stories—sports, events, clubs, awards, you name it. Any story that has anything to do with our school community is fair game. We also need opinion writers. If you have a viewpoint on a subject, other students want to hear about it. Am I missing anything, Dylan and Marissa?"

"Pictures!" both said in unison.

Mrs. Bronson laughed. "Of course. Pictures. Everyone loves to see their smiling faces in the paper, so let's get plenty of photos. Those of you who have phones also have cameras. Let's use them."

"Our first edition goes out two weeks from Friday," Dylan said. "That means we need to have everything in to Marissa and me no later than the end of school a week from Tuesday. That gives us two days to edit and do the layout. We print on Thursday nights and have the papers ready for students on Friday morning."

"For the new people, we'd like to get your story ideas by next Tuesday," Marissa added. "That's only a week from now, but don't sweat it. Right now, we're just looking for story ideas, not completed stories. Come up with as many as you can think of, even if you're not sure it's any good. Hopefully, that will give us a big list we can pick from for the next edition. Sound good?"

Stephanie timidly raised her hand. "I haven't done this before," she said. "Can I look through some papers from last year to get some ideas?"

"Good thinking," Marissa answered. "I'm sorry, what's your name again?"

"Stephanie."

"Good idea, Stephanie. We've got all the issues from last year online and should have printed copies in the newspaper office. That will give you a good feel for the kind of stories we're looking for."

Stephanie breathed a sigh of relief. She had absolutely no clue what she should write about. She looked around the room and saw a couple of kids from her English class who also looked a little nervous, which made her feel better.

"For you newcomers," Marissa continued, "we'll probably just assign you stories for the first couple of editions, but we want you to start thinking about your own ideas too. And don't worry if we don't choose your story concepts at first. You'll figure out the kinds of stories we're looking for and then you'll have lots of great ideas, I promise."

That night, Stephanie spent three hours reading through old editions of *Tyler Talk*. She took pages of notes

The Election Calculation

as she went through the first four editions, then less and less as she went on. She was a little disappointed there wasn't more variety in the stories. Most were a picture of a club activity and a short writeup of the event. The chess club competed in a four-school tournament. The seventh-grade basketball team went seven and six on the season. That story was accompanied by a blurry picture of Dylan Bridgers shooting a layup. There was a photo of academic award winners with their names listed underneath, a story about a teacher who was runner-up for teacher of the year (no mention of who won), and another about two students who volunteered with the Humane Society. The only thing close to a hard-hitting story was one about the cafeteria using food that was getting close to the expiration date. Most of the space in the paper was devoted to the monthly calendar, sports scores, a monthly article from the principal called "A View from the Office," and minutes from the bi-weekly school board meeting.

What did she want to write about? There had to be more out there than the chess club and basketball scores.

And then the thought hit her.

What about the math club? Was there a story in Kenny Hanley's total control of the club, his ability to single-handedly choose who was in and who was out?

Stephanie decided it might be a story worth writing, but she wasn't quite ready to present it to Dylan and Marissa yet.

Chapter 4

The next day was the first day of the math club.

"Okay, let's get started," Kenny said as he looked around the room. He frowned at the Math Kids sitting together by the windows. He took a quick glance at Buzz and two of his friends on the other side and rolled his eyes.

"Just so we're all clear on the purpose of this club," he continued. "We're here to win the state math tournament in the spring. We finished in third place last year, but we only missed the finals by a few points, so we were right there at the end."

"We'll get 'em this year," Buzz chimed in.

Kenny nodded. "Buzz is right. Parkview lost their best two people, and I think Belmont lost half their team. We've got everybody back, so we should be in good shape to win it all this year."

"And you've got some new team members this year," Jordan spoke up.

The Election Calculation

"We don't need any new team members," Kenny snarled. "We came within a couple of problems of taking state. Why would we risk that with new people with less experience?"

"Unless they were better, of course," Jordan said.

This comment drew angry stares from most of the people in the room. Stephanie glanced over at Jordan with a look that said, "What are you doing?"

"I think what Jordan was saying is that we do have experience," Stephanie said. "We won district last year."

Buzz laughed. "That was elementary school. That's the minor leagues. Besides, most of us won districts too. Not to brag, but our team won three years in a row." He stood and took an exaggerated bow as some of the other kids laughed and applauded.

"Well, I can speak from experience that these four are good," Josh Benson spoke up, waving his hand in the direction of the Math Kids. "They were the ones who beat us in districts last year and we had a really good team."

Stephanie smiled and mouthed "thank you" to him.

Kenny gave Josh a hard stare. "Oh, that's so sweet to stick up for your girlfriend."

Josh started to protest, but Kenny raised his hand. "Okay, that's enough interruptions. We've got a lot of work to do. To qualify for the state tournament, we have to be one of the top three teams in our region. Between now and the regional tournament, we'll work on problems both individually and in groups. You'll be expected to be here every Wednesday after school and to do homework problems in between meetings. Is that understood?"

He looked around at the nodding heads.

While Kenny was talking, Catherine looked across the room at the short redheaded girl sitting near the windows. The girl looked up at her and then quickly turned away. Trudy Hanley, Kenny's sister. She and Catherine had become friends in their summer robotics camp. Trudy was super smart and had always made Catherine laugh. She was also a traitor! When Catherine had confided in her that she and her friends thought Buzz and Kenny were stealing comics, Trudy had told her brother about the plans the Math Kids were making to catch them.

"Okay," Kenny said. "We'll be taking two teams to the regional tournament. Each team will have six players. The A team will only include players who have already competed in the tournament."

This statement brought frowns to a number of kids in the room, including Kenny's sister, who was also new to the math club this year.

Kenny ignored the looks and continued, "The B team will compete, but no one really expects them to win. They'll mostly use the tournament to learn from the better players. Now I'm sure you can do the math—if not, you're in the wrong place—but that means five of you will not make either of the teams. You'll be left behind when the rest of us go to the tournament."

His gaze lingered on Josh and the four Math Kids.

Jordan stared right back at him with a look of defiance. "Gosh, I wonder who the five will be," he said sarcastically.

Kenny gave him a broad smile and said, "As president of the math club, I'll make the final decision on who is on which team."

Kenny's words stuck in Justin's head, and he was still fuming when he and his friends walked out of school after math club ended.

"I still can't believe that jerk is going to stop us from competing," Justin seethed.

"Unfortunately, I think he probably will," Catherine said. "They might not be able to prevent us from joining the club, but if the president gets to choose who competes, we're out of luck."

"Like they say, it's good to be the king," Josh said as he joined the group.

"Well, if you ask me, this is a king who needs to be knocked off his throne," Jordan said.

"Yeah, good luck with that," Josh said. "He's got a lot of people on his side."

"There are five of us," Stephanie pointed out. "That's almost a third of the club."

"Unfortunately, it might be just four," Josh said. "I'm not sure if I'm going to be able to stay in the math club."

"How come?" Catherine asked.

"Basketball practice is at the same time as math club," Josh said. "I'm going to talk to the coach and see if I can come late to practice on Wednesdays, but I'm pretty sure he's going to say no. Besides, with that guy in charge, I don't think I'm going to miss it much."

"That's too bad," Stephanie said. "I mean, first of all, you stuck up for us in there, which we all appreciated."

"And second of all?" Josh prompted.

"Well, don't get a big head or anything, but you're also pretty good at math," Justin said.

"Yeah, I was looking forward to competing *with* you instead of *against* you this time," Josh said with a smile. "Anyway, I gotta go. My mom just got here. Good luck one way or the other."

"It just isn't fair," Stephanie said after Josh had left.

"Like Kenny said, who said life is fair?" Jordan said. "But maybe there *is* something we can do about it."

"Like what?" Justin countered. "Kenny's the president and he gets to make the rules."

"Maybe," Jordan said, "but we all know he's kind of a jerk. Maybe some others in the club feel that way too."

"Trudy sure didn't look happy when Kenny said she couldn't compete on the A team," Justin said.

"Who cares how Trudy feels?" Catherine asked, a hint of anger in her voice.

The Election Calculation

"You may not have noticed, but she kept looking at you the whole meeting," Jordan said. "I think she feels bad about what she did to you during the whole situation with the comic books."

"Hah!" Stephanie said scornfully. "I don't think she even knows how to feel bad."

"Maybe," Jordan said, "but if she did, she might just be able to convince a few other people that Kenny needs to go."

"I don't know," Stephanie said. "Even if we got Trudy to turn on her brother, that still leaves a lot more people on Kenny's side. Besides, I kind of understand why they don't want to change things up much. Their team did really well last year. Maybe they're better at math than we are."

"You may be right," Jordan admitted, "but—"

"What do you mean she might be right?" Justin interrupted. "How can you say that without even knowing how we'd do against them?"

Jordan waited for Justin to finish before continuing, "… but I think we should at least get a chance to prove that we're pretty good too."

"Okay, then," Justin said. "So how do we get our chance?"

"I don't know," Jordan said. "That's what we need to figure out."

Chapter 5

At the next meeting of the school newspaper, Stephanie didn't have much in the way of story ideas. She suggested a story on the experience of choosing a new club as a sixth grader. Unfortunately, Yasmin Aziz, another newspaper newbie, had come up with a similar story and was already working on a draft.

"Great idea, though, Stephanie," Marissa told her. "Great minds think alike, right?"

"I guess," Stephanie replied. "That was really all I came up with though. Sorry."

"No problem," Marissa said. She looked through a list of story ideas, many with checkmarks and names printed next to them to show they had already been assigned. "Okay, here's one. Could you go to the board meeting tonight and take some minutes? Kevin was going to go but he has the flu."

"Yeah, I could do that," Stephanie said, trying to keep the disappointment out of her voice. She had been to a board meeting before when she and Catherine had asked the board members if they could move the district math competition to a different date. Other than when they had been able to address the board, most of the meeting was dreadfully dull.

They should call them bored meetings, she thought, but she told herself she would write as good a story as she could. If Dylan and Marissa and Mrs. Bronson liked her writing, maybe they would give her more interesting stories in the future.

That evening, Stephanie's mom dropped her off twenty minutes before the start of the board meeting.

"I'll pick you up at eight-thirty," her mom said. She waved and drove off.

Stephanie entered the administration building and sat in a folding chair by the aisle about halfway back. She pulled her notebook and a pen out of her purse and waited for the crowd to arrive. It didn't. Only a few people wandered into the room and took seats. Stephanie took a quick count of the crowd as the meeting began. Thirteen people, including herself.

Pretty poor showing—only 13 people, she jotted down in her notebook.

She carefully wrote down the names of the seven board members.

President — Mr. Bilson
Vice President — Mrs. Guidry
Secretary — Mrs. Franklin

Treasurer — Mr. Santosh
Board Member — Mrs. Carmichael
Board Member — Mrs. Livingston
Board Member — Mrs. Howard

A few chairs over, a dark-haired young man in jeans and a sport coat was also taking notes. He nodded at Stephanie and then reached into a pocket. He leaned over to hand her a business card. Stephanie glanced at the card. Bill Blankenship, investigative reporter for The Maynard Gazette. Now Stephanie didn't feel so bad. *I guess even investigative reporters get stuck covering school board meetings*, she thought, before turning her attention back to the front of the room.

Mr. Bilson brought the meeting to order. The red-haired secretary—Stephanie took a note that she should get her name at the end of the meeting—read the minutes from the previous meeting. The board moved on to old business. There was a lengthy discussion about the new performing arts center. Stephanie wrote as quickly as she could as they spoke, trying to capture as much of the conversation as possible. The performing arts center had been new business when she and Catherine had spoken at the board meeting, but now it seemed the proposal had progressed to the point that they were discussing taking bids on the construction.

The Election Calculation

Mr. Santosh, the board treasurer, expressed some concerns about the overall cost.

Mrs. Guidry wrinkled her nose every time Mr. Santosh spoke, obviously not agreeing with anything he said. "This is an opportunity for this board to make a lasting impression on this school district," she countered.

"That's fine," he said, "but we still need to be fiscally responsible."

Several other board members chimed in with their thoughts and Stephanie wrote furiously, trying her best to keep up.

Finally, Mr. Bilson brought the discussion to a close with a raised hand. "Okay, great discussion everyone, but we do need to move on to new business if we're going to finish the meeting by eight-thirty."

Mrs. Guidry looked like she was going to say something else, but instead just frowned and shook her head.

There wasn't much new business, just a reminder that the school board elections were coming up. Mr. Bilson, Mr. Santosh, and Mrs. Carmichael's terms were expiring. Stephanie noted that all three were on the ballot for the election.

"Now we'll open up the floor for public comments," Mr. Bilson said. "Please line up at the microphone in the center aisle, and I'd ask you to limit your time to three minutes so that everyone will have a chance to speak."

Stephanie smiled. With only thirteen people in the audience, it didn't look like getting to everyone's comments would be a problem.

Two teachers expressed concerns about the new math books in the elementary schools. The board members nodded but didn't comment. When it looked like no one else was going to speak, Stephanie closed her notebook and prepared to leave. At the last moment, a man in a grey suit approached the microphone.

"Good evening," he said in a smooth voice. "I'm Samuel Woodley. I'm running for the school board."

"I wasn't aware of any other candidates," Mr. Bilson responded.

Mr. Woodley smiled. "Perfectly understandable," he said, "as my slate of candidates will be formally submitting our names as candidates tomorrow morning."

"Your slate?" Mr. Bilson raised an eyebrow. Mr. Santosh and Mrs. Carmichael sat forward on their chairs and watched Mr. Woodley carefully.

"Yes," he answered. "I'll be running alongside Rebecca Tomlin and Thomas Patrick. We feel that we can more effectively bring about change through a team effort. You'll be hearing much more about our platform soon, but I wanted to take the opportunity to introduce myself."

He nodded at the board members and returned to his seat.

The Election Calculation

Stephanie watched the board to see their reaction. Mrs. Guidry was smiling broadly, while the other board members had furrowed brows and tight lips. Stephanie noted their expressions in her notebook.

She had not been looking forward to covering the board meeting. Now she couldn't wait for the next one. Maybe this was a story after all.

Chapter 6

"Okay, let's get started," Kenny said from the front of the math club room the next day after school. He scowled as he looked at the Math Kids sitting together again. Jordan grinned back as if to say "you're not going to get rid of us that easily," but he noticed that Josh Benson wasn't there, and that meant they had lost one of their only allies.

"As most of you know, except maybe the newcomers," Kenny continued, "there is a new format for the final round of the math competition this year."

At this, Jordan and his friends leaned forward and listened carefully. Kenny was right. This was new information for them.

"The final round will consist of six problems solved in series. The first person will have to solve a problem. The solution to that problem will be needed for the second person to solve their problem. The second person's solution will be needed for the third person, and so on."

The Election Calculation

"If the first person gets their problem wrong, we're done then, aren't we?" asked a boy with stringy blond hair.

"That's right, Mike," Kenny answered. "Each person won't be able to correctly solve their problem without the right information from the person in front of them."

Stephanie raised her hand. Kenny looked in her direction but ignored her. He pointed at his sister Trudy, who had also raised her hand.

"How does the scoring work?" asked Trudy.

Stephanie put her hand down as that was the question she was going to ask anyway.

"The team that gets the final question correct in the fastest time will win."

"But what if neither team gets it right?"

"If neither team gets it right or the time runs out, then the team that got furthest along the chain of problems with the right answers is the winner," Kenny explained.

"So what's the strategy?" Justin asked. "Does it make sense to put the best people up front to make sure you get further along than the other team?"

Kenny shot a look of annoyance at Justin. "Why does it matter to you, since the closest you're getting to the competition is sharpening my pencil?"

The classroom erupted into laughter. Justin's face turned scarlet. He started to get up, but Stephanie placed a hand gently on his arm.

Mr. Cosgrove, the math club sponsor, looked up from a stack of quizzes he was grading in the back of the room. He frowned at what he had just heard but remained silent.

"In answer to that question, Buzz and I are working on a strategy. Yes, we want to make sure we get a good start, but the problems are likely to get harder at the end of the problem set, so we'll probably put our very best at the back end. As president, I'll decide the order in which we go," Kenny said. "Now, let's get some practice in. Buzz, you want to get the teams set up?"

"Sure, Kenny," Buzz replied. "For this problem set, the first team will be me, Kenny, Mike, Bao, Phil, and Atiksh. The second team will be Trudy, Lucas, Maryam, Lei, Deiondre, and Oliver."

Buzz took a long look at the four who had not yet been called. Jordan returned his look with steady gaze.

"Sorry, guys, but I guess some of you will have to double up on problems since there are only four of you." He smirked. "Let me know if you need any help on any of the problems."

Buzz handed a stack of numbered envelopes to Oliver to distribute to his team. He kept a pile for himself. The rest he tossed onto a desk a few rows in front of Jordan and his friends.

"Thanks, Buzz," Jordan said, his voice dripping with unveiled sarcasm.

"We have forty-five minutes," Kenny said. "The clock starts now."

The Election Calculation

The Math Kids huddled in the front corner of the room.

"Okay, what's our strategy?" Jordan asked.

"I'll take the first problem," Stephanie said. "Catherine, why don't you take number two?"

"I'll take number three," Jordan added. "Justin, you can take number four."

"What do Jordan and I do while you two are solving your problems?" Justin asked.

"Look over your problem," Stephanie replied. "I think you'll be able to get started figuring it out without having our answers yet. When Catherine and I get done with our problems and pass them on to you, we'll start on number five and six. Sound like a plan?"

"Works for me," Jordan said.

"Remember to double-check your answer before handing it off to the next person," Justin said. "Once we get one wrong, we're done for."

"Good point, Justin," Stephanie agreed. "Okay, let's get started!"

Stephanie tore open her envelope and read the problem.

Problem 1:

I need to bring one hundred six cupcakes to the school bake sale. I bought two packages with eight cupcakes each. All the rest of the packages only had four cupcakes each. How many of these packages do I need to buy?

When you have solved the problem, give your answer to the person solving Problem 2.

> Wait! Do you want to try to solve this problem before Stephanie?
>
> **I need to bring one hundred cupcakes to the school bake sale. I bought two packages with eight cupcakes each. All the rest of the packages only had four cupcakes each. How many of these packages do I need to buy?**

Stephanie carefully read the problem, making sure she knew what question was being asked. She didn't want to get the team off on the wrong foot because, as Justin said, one mistake and it was all over.

She needed one hundred six cupcakes. She had two packages with eight cupcakes each. That was sixteen cupcakes.

She subtracted 16 from 106 to get 90 cupcakes that she still needed to buy.

Dividing 90 by 4 gave her 22 ½ packages.

Since she had to buy full packages, that meant she had to buy 23 of the four-packs of cupcakes.

She checked the math and decided it was as easy as that. She wrote 23 on a piece of paper and handed it to Catherine.

"Done already?" Catherine asked in surprise.

Stephanie nodded.

The Election Calculation

"Confident?"

"One hundred percent," Stephanie replied. "I'm going to take a look at problem five."

Catherine reread her problem.

Problem 2:

You will need to answer Problem 1 before proceeding.

The answer from Problem 1 falls between two numbers in the Fibonacci sequence. What are those two numbers?

When you have solved the problem, give the two numbers to the person solving Problem 3.

Catherine smiled. Her father had taught her the Fibonacci sequence several years ago. He had even used it to send her a coded message when he had been kidnapped. The pattern started with the numbers one and one.

1, 1

Each new element in the sequence was formed by adding the two previous numbers together. To get the third number, she just added one and one to get two.

1, 1, 2

She continued the sequence until she got past the number twenty-three provided by Stephanie from problem one.

1, 1, 2, 3, 5, 8, 13, 21, 34

Since 23 was in between 21 and 34, that was the answer she needed. She wrote 21 and 34 on a piece of paper and passed it to Jordan.

"Two down," she said with a smile.

Jordan nodded and looked again at his problem.

Problem 3:

You will need to answer Problem 2 before proceeding.

Combine the numbers from Problem 2 into a single number (for example, if you are given 8 and 24, combine them to make the number 824).

The resulting number is the product of three prime numbers. What are those three numbers?

When you have solved the problem, give the three numbers to the person solving Problem 4.

The Election Calculation

> Wait! Do you want to try to solve this problem before Stephanie?
>
> 2134 is the product of three prime numbers. What are those numbers?

Jordan stared at the number but wasn't sure where to start. There were probably hundreds of prime numbers that might evenly divide into 2134. Where should he even begin?

He was beginning to think he would have to tell Stephanie he didn't have the answers she would need for her next puzzle when he remembered that two was the only even prime number. Since 2134 was an even number, that meant two must be one of the divisors. Using some scratch paper, he wrote:

2134/2 = 1067

Okay, it was divisible by two. Now he just needed to figure out two prime numbers that multiplied to 1067. Not knowing a better way to proceed, he thought he would just start working through each of the prime numbers to see if he could find one that divided evenly into 1067.

Three was the next prime number. Jordan remembered there was an easy way to determine if a number was divisible by three. If the sum of the digits of the number was divisible by three, then the number was also divisible by three. He added the digits of 1067.

$1 + 0 + 6 + 7 = 14$

Since fourteen was not divisible by three, neither was 1067.

The next prime number after three was five. That was an easy one. All numbers divisible by five ended in either zero or five. Since 1067 didn't end in either zero or five, it wasn't divisible by five.

On to number seven. Jordan thought there was a rule to determine if a number was divisible by seven, but he couldn't remember it. He did a quick division using seven and found it didn't divide evenly into 1067. What was the next prime number? Eleven.

This time Jordan did remember the rule for figuring out if a number was divisible by eleven. It was like the rule for three, but instead of adding, you had to alternatively add and subtract the digits and see if that calculation yielded a number divisible by eleven. He did this with the digits of 1067.

$1 - 0 + 6 - 7 = 0$

Since 0 was divisible by 11, so was 1067! He divided 1067 by 11 and got 97.

The Election Calculation

That was it! He knew 97 was a prime number, so he had three prime numbers—2, 11, and 97—whose product was 2134.

He checked the clock. They were down to two minutes. There was no way they could do the last two problems in time.

"I'm sorry, guys," Jordan told his teammates. "I was too slow."

"It's alright," Justin said. "We got through four problems. That's not too bad for just getting started. I bet we did as well as the other teams."

"Done!" yelled Kenny.

"Us too!" said Oliver. "You just barely beat us!"

"But we did beat you," Buzz reminded him.

Kenny glanced over at Justin, who looked very dejected. "From the look on shorty's face, I guess the new kids failed the test."

"We only had four people," Justin shot back. "And even with only four of us, we still didn't do too bad."

"But you didn't get the final answer, did you?" Kenny asked.

"No, but—"

"Actually, we did," Catherine interrupted and held up a sheet of paper. "In fact, we had the answer about ten minutes ago."

"Oh yeah?" Buzz challenged. "Prove it!"

"The answer to the sixth puzzle is zero," she said.

The expression on Kenny's face said it all. Catherine was right!

Justin looked at Catherine in amazement. Lowering his voice to a whisper, he asked, "But how could you come up with the answer to problem six without knowing the answer to problem five?"

"It turns out I didn't need it," she replied. "Here, take a look."

Justin read problem six.

Problem 6:

If the three hundredth number in the Fibonacci sequence is odd, multiply the answer to Problem 5 by five. If the three hundredth number is even, multiply the answer to Problem 5 by zero.

What is the final answer?

"Let us see too," Stephanie said, trying to look over Justin's shoulder at the question. Justin handed her the problem and she and Jordan read it.

"Did you just take a guess the Fibonacci number was even?" Jordan asked. "I mean, there's no way you calculated all three hundred numbers in like five minutes."

"I didn't have to," Catherine said with a smile.

"You found a pattern, didn't you?" Stephanie asked.

The Election Calculation

Catherine nodded. She started to explain, but Stephanie held up her hand. "Wait a minute, let me try first."

Stephanie wrote the first few digits in the sequence.

1, 1, 2, 3, 5, 8, 13, 21, 34 …

This time she paid attention to whether the digits were even or odd. It didn't take her long to spot the pattern.

odd, odd, even, odd, odd, even, odd, odd, even …

"Every third number is even," she said.

Now Jordan saw it. "It makes sense," he said. "If we got two even numbers in a row, all the rest of the numbers after that would have to be even, so the only time we're going to get an even number is when we add two odd numbers together."

"And that only happens every third number," Justin added.

"And the three hundredth number is going to be one of those numbers," Catherine said.

"Nice work," Stephanie said, patting her friend on her back.

"It doesn't matter," Kenny said loudly. "Just because you were lucky enough to get the final answer, you never finished problem five, so it doesn't count."

"Actually, it does," Mr. Cosgrove said from the back of the room. He rose to his feet and walked to the front of the room, pausing as he passed Catherine to give her a nod of approval.

"You said it yourself, Kenny," he continued. "The team that correctly answers the final problem in the shortest amount of time wins. I purposefully structured this set of problems so you could figure out the final answer without knowing the answer to any of the other problems. In fact, the statement from problem six doesn't say you need to answer problem five before proceeding. Catherine was the first one to figure that out."

"But she never said she had the answer!" Buzz protested.

"I wanted to give Stephanie time to work on problem five," Catherine said. "I mean, this is practice, right?"

Mr. Cosgrove nodded. "Correct, this is practice."

"But shouldn't we be practicing to win?" Kenny countered.

"No, we should be practicing working together as a team," Mr. Cosgrove replied. "Being competitive at the tournament is fine, but in this room we're all on the same team. Let's try to remember that." He gave Kenny a long look and then glanced at his watch. "Okay, we're out of time. There are some sample problems on the front desk. Take a packet to work on this week. See you next Wednesday."

Chapter 7

Jordan and his friends waited in the circle drive in front of the school. His mom had promised to pick them up after math club. They were all smiles after Catherine had answered the final question and Mr. Cosgrove had chastised Kenny and his cohorts for not being team players.

"Something funny?" Kenny growled as he approached.

"Nope," Jordan said, deciding that it wasn't worth engaging with the bigger boy.

"You got lucky today, red," he said to Catherine.

She shook her head at the insulting way he said "red." It was funny because Kenny and his sister both had bright orange hair, so teasing Catherine about her red hair didn't really make any sense. "People who live in glass houses shouldn't throw stones," she said.

Kenny glared. "I should just throw you out of the math club."

"I don't think Mr. Cosgrove would allow that," Stephanie replied.

"You're probably right, but there's nothing he can do to stop me from leaving you out of the competition. It says so right in the club handbook—the president has final say over who competes."

"Does it say anything about the president having to be a jerk?" Jordan asked.

Kenny took a menacing step in his direction, then stopped as Jordan's mom pulled into the circle.

"Sorry," Jordan said. "I guess we'll have to finish this conversation another day." He and his friends quickly hopped into the car and Jordan's mom drove away.

Stephanie looked out of the back window and saw Kenny was staring after them, his fists clenched and his face almost as red as his hair.

"How was math club?" Jordan's mom asked.

"You know, we just worked on some math problems," Jordan answered, leaving out all the drama that had played out with Kenny.

Stephanie caught the clue and added, "The problems are harder, but I think it's going to be fun. I really like Mr. Cosgrove."

"Sounds great," Jordan's mom said as she slowed to a halt at a stop sign.

While they waited for the cross traffic to pass, Stephanie looked out of the window. Her eyebrows raised as she saw a large yard sign. It was white with bold, blue letters stating, *Building a Brighter Future, One Student at a Time.* Beneath the tagline were three names in red: *Woodley, Tomlin, Patrick.* Stephanie quickly pulled out her notebook and scribbled down the wording on the sign. In the next ten minutes, she saw three more signs, each with a different slogan.

Dedicated to a Better Education for All

Empowering Education for a Better Future

Working Together for a Better Education System

Each statement went into her notebook. It might make a good addition to her story on the school board meeting.

"What do you keep writing down?" Justin asked.

Stephanie explained her visit to the school board and Mr. Woodley's announcement that he and two others were running as a slate for the school board.

"They're running, alright," Mrs. Waters laughed. "Their signs are everywhere. They must be putting a lot of money into this election. The funny thing is no one seems to know who they are."

"That's it!" Stephanie exclaimed.

"What's it?" Jordan asked.

"We don't like the way Kenny runs things, right?" Stephanie looked at the nods of agreement from her friends before continuing. "And the only way to change that is to elect a new president."

"And just who were you thinking about for the new president?" Justin asked.

"It doesn't really matter, does it?" Stephanie reasoned.

"I mean, anyone would be better. Well, maybe not Buzz, but you know what I mean."

"Yeah, but how do we convince the kids in the club to elect someone else?" Catherine asked.

"Well, the way I figure it, except for Buzz, Kenny, and Trudy, no one in the math club knows who we are," Stephanie said. "If we want to convince people there is a better alternative to Kenny, they need to know who we are first."

"I guess that makes sense," Jordan said. "So what are you proposing?"

"We need to get out there and meet the other kids in the math club," Stephanie said.

"We need a name," Justin said.

"A name for what?" Jordan asked.

"Our operation," Justin said.

Stephanie giggled. Justin always felt the need to call every plan by some name.

"What about Operation Popularity?" Justin suggested.

"Operation Popularity?" Catherine asked dubiously.

Justin grinned. "Yeah, but we could call it Op Pop for short."

Stephanie groaned but smiled. "Okay, Op Pop it is."

They put the Op Pop plan into action the next day at school. They decided it was best to split up so they could reach out to more people.

The Election Calculation

At lunchtime, Jordan spotted Deiondre sitting alone at a table, chewing slowly while he read a comic book.

"You sitting with anybody?" Jordan asked.

Deiondre looked around the table, which was clearly empty except for himself. "It's a free country," he said.

It was not exactly an invitation, but Jordan sat across from him anyway.

"What are you reading?" Jordan asked.

Deiondre lifted his gaze from the comic book and stared curiously at Jordan. "What do you want?"

"I don't want anything," Jordan said. "It's just that we're in the same club and I thought I should get to know my teammates."

"Teammates?" Deiondre asked. "It doesn't sound like you and your friends are going to be on anyone's team. I don't know what you did to Buzz and Kenny, but they sure don't like you guys."

"It's a long story," Jordan started to explain, but he was interrupted by Deiondre rising from his seat.

"Look, dude, I'm not getting in the middle of this," he said. "If you've got a problem with Kenny, you should take it up with him. Just leave me out of it." Deiondre grabbed his tray and walked away.

Jordan watched Deiondre go, then opened his lunch bag. He pulled out a sandwich and some grapes. He reached for the container at the bottom of the bag, hoping for cookies but was disappointed to find carrots and celery. *It looks like I'm not even popular with my mom today.*

On the other side of the cafeteria, Justin was trying his luck with Lucas and Oliver, who were deep in conversation at a table against the wall.

"Hey guys," he said in greeting. The two boys looked up at him warily.

"Yeah?" Oliver asked.

"I was hoping we could talk about a couple of the problems for next week while we eat," Justin said, reaching into his backpack for the problem set.

"No way," Lucas said. "You just want us to give you the answers."

"No, I think I got most of them," Justin explained, which wasn't exactly true. In reality, he had worked out all the problems as soon as he got home from math club and had even checked his answers with Jordan.

"Well, keep working then," Oliver said, turning his attention back to Lucas.

"Yeah, okay," Justin replied. "So, how do you guys feel about the way Kenny runs the math club?"

Both Lucas and Oliver ignored the question and continued their conversation, speaking in low tones. Justin walked away in frustration. He saw Jordan sitting by himself and plopped down on a seat across from him.

The Election Calculation

"How'd it go with Deiondre?" Justin asked.

Jordan shook his head. "Not good. Lucas and Oliver?"

"Wouldn't give me the time of day," Justin said. "Op Pop is going to be harder than I thought."

"Tell me about it," Jordan said. He grabbed another carrot and took a crunchy bite.

"You're eating carrots?" Justin asked in amazement.

"Yeah, but not on purpose," Jordan replied sadly.

"I hope Stephanie and Catherine are having better luck than we did," Justin said.

"Yeah, and I hoped my mom would give me cookies instead of carrots, and look how that turned out," Jordan responded.

In homeroom, Stephanie had decided to talk to Maryam Heydari, another of the sixth graders new to the math club.

"Hi, Maryam," Stephanie said as she slid into the chair next to Maryam.

"Hello," Maryam said. "Your name is Stephanie, right?"

"That's me," Stephanie replied.

"Did you really find hidden treasure?" Maryam asked.

"My friends and I did," Stephanie admitted. "It was a team effort, and we had to use math to do it."

"That's pretty cool," Maryam said.

"What elementary school did you come from?" Stephanie asked.

"It wasn't around here," Maryam answered. "My family just moved to Maynard this summer."

"Well, welcome," Stephanie said. "I only moved here a couple of years ago, but I really like it so far. How about you?"

"It's all very new," Maryam said. "It's a big school and it's hard to meet new people with all of the moving between classes."

"Yeah, same here," Stephanie said. "Well, at least you'll get to know the kids in the math club. We all stay in one place."

"I don't know about math club," Maryam admitted. "I know a lot about math, but I don't know if I'm good enough to compete. I guess that's for Kenny to decide."

"That's what I wanted to talk to you about." Stephanie knew she had to be careful with what she said next. Trying to keep her voice as neutral as possible, she asked, "What do you think about Kenny?"

"I don't know him very well," Maryam said, "but his sister Trudy is very nice, so I guess he is okay too."

That wasn't what Stephanie wanted to hear. "You don't think it's unfair that the new kids don't get to try out for the first team?" Stephanie asked.

"Oh, no," Maryam said. "I'm glad Kenny is going to put me on the second team so I can learn more."

Stephanie's heart sank. While Maryam seemed very nice, everything she said indicated she would probably go along with anything Kenny said.

So far, Op Pop was off to a dismal start. Stephanie,

The Election Calculation

Jordan, and Justin had struck out. That only left Catherine to make any progress, and she had the toughest job of all. She had to reach out to Trudy, the girl who had already shown she would put her brother above her friends.

Catherine saw Trudy in the hallway after her final class of the day. Trudy was talking to a couple of girls while she put some books into her locker. Catherine waited until the other girls said goodbye and walked away before she tentatively approached.

"Hey, Trudy," Catherine said.

Trudy spun around, startled to find Catherine standing behind her.

"What do you want?" Trudy asked.

"Just to talk, I guess," Catherine said.

"About what?"

"Well, I was hoping we could maybe start over," Catherine said.

"After what you did to me?"

"What I did to you?" Catherine said in astonishment. "You were supposed to be my friend and you betrayed me."

"Yeah, well what about me?" Trudy asked. "You put our friendship in between me and my brother.

"I didn't even know he was your brother at the time," Catherine protested.

"You and your friends got my brother banned from the mall, and now my parents won't let me go either."

"I'm sorry about that, but that was Kenny's fault, not

ours!" Catherine fired back, her face reddening in anger. "He and Buzz were the ones who were stealing the comic books and they blamed it on Justin. I'm glad Kenny got banned from the mall."

"But he's my brother."

"And Justin is my friend," Catherine said. "Look, I don't have a brother, so I admit I don't know what you were going through. But I do know this; sometimes you have to make difficult decisions. I made mine, and I'm sticking with it." She turned and walked away, leaving Trudy standing at her locker.

Chapter 8

At breakfast the next morning, Stephanie brought up the school board election with her mom.

"Have you seen all the signs for the new candidates?" Stephanie asked.

"It's kind of hard to miss them," her mom replied.

"Mrs. Waters said she hadn't heard of them before the signs. Is that strange?"

"Well, usually someone running for the board has some connection with the district, like they're an ex-teacher or administrator or they have kids in the district," her mom replied. "But it's like these three came out of nowhere."

"So it is strange," Stephanie said. She gave her ponytail a little tug as she thought about it. What was their connection to the school district?

"What are you two talking about?" Stephanie's dad asked as he came into the kitchen and filled his coffee cup.

"The new candidates running for the school board," Stephanie answered.

Her dad rolled his eyes. "You mean the sign people?"

The Election Calculation

"Yeah, I saw four of their signs on the way home from school," Stephanie said.

"Only four?" her dad asked. "I bet I saw at least a dozen. They're everywhere."

"Why do you think they have so many?" Stephanie asked.

"Because, unfortunately, that's what wins," her dad answered. "You see, a lot of people don't put much thought into a school board election. All they remember is what names they saw on a sign. The more signs, the better the chance people will vote for them on election day."

"Well, they must be spending a fortune," her mom said as she spooned sugar into her cup of tea.

"Why would someone spend so much to be on the school board?" Stephanie asked.

"There are only two reasons I've ever seen anyone run for office," her dad said. "The first is to do something to make things better for everyone else. The second is to do something to make things better for themselves. I know that sounds cynical, but I've seen it time and time again."

"But why the school board?" Stephanie asked. "I mean, do they ever vote on anything important?"

Her dad smiled. "They do, although lots of people don't think about that. The school board controls the budget for the entire school district. For our district, that's in the tens of millions of dollars, but for some very large districts, that number might be in the billions."

"Billions?"

"Yep, billions with a B," her dad said.

"That's a lot of money," Stephanie exclaimed.

"It sure is," her dad said. "And sometimes politicians want to get their hands on some of it."

"That's illegal, isn't it?" Stephanie asked.

"It is, but that doesn't always stop them," her dad said. He took another sip of coffee.

"Why so many questions about the election?" her mom asked.

"I'm thinking about doing a story on these new candidates," Stephanie said. "I'm just not sure where to start."

"My recommendation is to follow the money," her dad said.

"Follow the money?" Stephanie asked.

"Follow the money," her dad repeated. "What's in it for them? Those signs are probably costing them thousands of dollars. They wouldn't spend it unless they thought it was somehow worth it. So ... follow the money."

Stephanie finished her breakfast in silence, thoughts spinning through her head. What started as a boring visit to the school board meeting was now getting interesting. She needed to talk to Mrs. Bronson about pursuing this new story.

✷✷✷

The Election Calculation

"It sounds like a great story," Stephanie's English teacher told her when she brought up her idea. "Be sure to let Dylan and Marissa know about it."

Stephanie worked on her story idea all weekend. She remembered Mrs. Bronson had told them about the five W's when writing a story.

Who is the story about? That one was easy. The story would be about the mysterious slate of characters running for the school board. Who were Samuel Woodley, Rebecca Tomlin, and Thomas Patrick?

Where did it happen? Another easy one. It was in the school district. But she also wrote down a note that it might be important to know where they came from if they were new to the district.

When is it happening? Right now. The three were officially running now, and the election was only a few weeks away.

What is happening? At first glance, this was an easy question. The *what* was that they were running for school board. But Stephanie thought there might be more to the *what*. And it had to do with the toughest question, the one she had no clue about right now.

***Why** is it happening?* Why were the three running for school board? Her dad had asked "what was in it for them?" The *why* and the *what* seemed to blur a little. Stephanie jotted down some questions she needed to get answered:

> **What is the school district budget? Can I get this from Mr. Santosh, the school board treasurer?**
>
> **How long have the three candidates been in the district?**
>
> **Do their kids go to school in the district?**
>
> **Have any of the candidates worked in the district?**

Stephanie reviewed her list of questions. The last three would probably have to be answered by the candidates themselves. She wondered how she could go about setting up an interview with them.

By Tuesday, she had her story idea written up in some detail. She was proud of her effort to get things put into order and was well prepared to answer any questions Dylan and Marissa would have for her.

What she wasn't prepared for was Mrs. Bronson, who asked her to stay behind at the end of her English class.

"You wanted to see me, Mrs. Bronson?" she asked when her classmates had finally cleared the room.

The Election Calculation

"Yes, Stephanie," her teacher said.

There was a long pause as she pondered what to say. The wait made Stephanie nervous. Finally, her teacher spoke, cautiously picking out the exact words she wanted to say.

"I'm afraid I can't give you permission to pursue your story on the three candidates running for the school board," she began.

"But you said it was a great idea," Stephanie said.

"I did say that, and I still think it's a great idea, but I can't give you permission to do it. The administration usually doesn't approve stories about school board elections. Those are their bosses after all."

"So I can't do the story?"

"I didn't say that," Mrs. Bronson said carefully. "I said I can't give you permission to pursue the story."

"I'm confused, Mrs. Bronson," Stephanie said.

"Let me tell you a story, Stephanie. Once there was a village whose well had run dry. In this village there lived a smart young woman who knew that if she dug a canal from the nearby stream, the village would have all the water they needed. Unfortunately, the only way to get to the stream was through the field of a wealthy landowner. The young woman knew she would never get the landowner's permission, so she waited until it was dark and then dug the canal. The water flowed to the village and the problem was solved."

"But wasn't the landowner mad?"

"Absolutely furious," Mrs. Bronson said. "But, when the young woman apologized and explained why she did it, the landowner forgave her and allowed the canal to remain. The young woman became a hero in the village because she didn't let obstacles stand in her way. She just did what she knew was the right thing to do."

Stephanie nodded thoughtfully, trying to get where her teacher was going with the story.

"Are you're saying that it's easier to ask for forgiveness than it is to get permission?"

"That's what the story is saying," Mrs. Bronson said. "What I'm saying is I can't give you permission to pursue the story."

Stephanie started to say something, but her teacher raised a hand to stop her. "You'd better be getting to your next class. If you're looking for something to do after school, though, I heard that the election office has the names and addresses of everyone running for the school board."

She smiled at Stephanie and turned to erase the whiteboard in preparation for her next class.

At lunch, Stephanie and Catherine discussed the cryptic conversation with Mrs. Bronson.

"What do you think she was trying to tell me?" Stephanie asked.

The Election Calculation

Catherine prepared her food while she thought. Her dad had packed her sushi for lunch. She tore open two packets of soy sauce and used chop sticks to mix in a dab of wasabi. She dipped a spicy tuna roll into the mixture and popped it into her mouth. She savored the delicious bite before answering.

"Well, it definitely sounds like she wants you to do the story," she said.

"Yeah, but who is telling her I can't do it? The principal?" Stephanie asked.

"Or maybe someone even higher," Catherine said.

"Who's higher than the principal?"

Catherine shrugged and grabbed another tuna roll with her chopsticks. She dipped it and placed it into her mouth. She chewed thoughtfully.

"The story is about the school board," she said. "Do you think maybe they don't want anyone looking into the election?"

"But why?" Stephanie asked.

"That's the real question."

"I think it's more than the real question," Stephanie said. "I think it's the real story," Stephanie said. "Well, permission or not, I'm going to look into this."

"I wouldn't have expected anything else," Catherine said with a smile. "What's your next step?"

"I'm going to pay a visit to the election office and find out more about these three new candidates."

Chapter 9

Jordan peeked in the door of the classroom. The lights were off, and the window shades were down, the room lit solely by the glow of video screens. In front of each screen huddled anywhere from one to four kids holding game controllers, each intent on the flickering image before them. Jordan smiled as he picked out Justin, who was moving his body left and right as he used his controller to fend off a horde of zombies threatening to overtake his position. Justin blinked and looked around as the overhead lights came on.

"Hey, turn off the lights!" he objected.

"Sorry guys, it's time to shut down the games," Mr. Jacobs said.

There were groans and protests, but save icons were pressed and game consoles switched off amid loud discussions of which team had outplayed the other. Justin finally noticed Jordan was waiting for him and slid his controller into his overstuffed backpack. He waved a hand at the room in general as he left with his friend.

The Election Calculation

"Looks like you guys were really going at it," Jordan said as they walked down the hall.

"Yeah, Albert brought in his new version of *Zombie Battle*. You would not believe the graphics. It was so real-life."

"Um, if zombies were real," Jordan teased.

"Well, yeah, but it was so realistic I thought they were for a while."

"Sounds cool."

"It is. I need to find a way to talk my parents into getting it for me for my birthday."

"Your birthday isn't for eleven months," Jordan pointed out.

"I didn't think about that. You think they'd get it for me for a Halloween present?"

"I doubt it," Jordan said.

"You're probably right. Oh well, it doesn't hurt to try. It's a really cool game. How was your club, by the way?"

"It was good," Jordan said without providing any details.

"You still haven't told me what club you chose," Justin said.

"I guess you're right."

"First you learn how to play the violin without me ever knowing about it and now you're in some secret club. Why all the secrecy?"

"It's not really a secret," Jordan said. "I guess I just didn't want you to make fun of me."

"You're my best friend. Would I ever make fun of you?"

Jordan stopped and gave his friend a long look. Justin laughed and said, "Okay, so I occasionally make fun of you. That's what friends do. So spill it. What club are you in?"

"I'm in the cooking club," Jordan said.

"Are you serious?" Justin laughed.

"See? That's why I didn't want to tell you."

"I'm not laughing at you," Justin said. "I mean, yeah, I laughed, but not because I'm making fun of you. It's just that it's such a perfect club for you. I've never seen anyone who thinks about food more than you do, so why not learn to cook it?"

"Right? And the best part is that we get to eat what we make. It's kind of like a pre-dinner snack. Today we made the best mac and cheese I've ever had. None of that stuff from a box, you know, with that powdery orange junk they call cheese. This was real cheese that we grated ourselves. It came out in these long strips of deliciousness just waiting to be melted onto those noodles. Man, it was so good."

Justin laughed at the earnestness of his friend describing macaroni and cheese.

While Jordan's mom drove them home, they put video games and food behind them and concentrated on the problem of the math club. Jordan dug through his backpack and came up with a crumpled booklet.

The Election Calculation

"What's that?"

"It's the math club handbook," Jordan answered. "I figured it would be better to read it ourselves rather than take Kenny's word for it."

"Good idea. I don't trust anything that guy says."

"And here's exactly what we were looking for," Jordan said. He opened the booklet to page six and pointed out the heading to Jordan. "Elections. It turns out we are supposed to have an election within the first six meetings of the math club each year, but if no one calls for an election, the current president retains his position without even having a vote."

"That doesn't seem fair."

"It isn't. But guess who wrote the handbook?"

"Let me guess. Kenny?"

"Exactly. The date on the handbook is last year. I bet he's hoping that no one calls for an election and he can just keep being president."

"That sounds like Kenny," Justin said. "And no one is going to do it because of the power Kenny holds with choosing the competition teams. If someone calls for an election, Kenny might kick them off the team."

"Exactly," Jordan replied. "That means it's up to us to do it since we have nothing to lose anyway."

"But it's not going to matter, is it? We don't have the votes to beat him."

"Not in a traditional election, but it turns out there are

lots of different ways to vote and the handbook doesn't specify which one we have to use. We just need to figure out which one would work for us and talk Kenny into using that kind of voting method."

"It sounds like we need a meeting of the Math Kids," Justin said.

While Justin and Jordan were discussing mac and cheese and elections, Stephanie's dad was dropping her off at the county administration office. She looked up at the three-story brick building with its walls of tinted glass. Taking a deep breath, she entered through the double doors to find a beautiful lobby lined with offices. She went to the registration desk and asked for directions to the elections office.

"Second floor. First door on the right. Elevators are behind me," the woman behind the desk told her without looking up.

Stephanie entered the elevator and pushed the button for the second floor. Following the woman's directions, she took the first door on the right. Inside, there was another desk, this one lined with stacks of forms and a plastic basket of ink pens.

"Can I help you?" asked a balding man with squinty eyes sitting behind the desk. Stephanie glanced down at his computer screen and saw he was in the middle of a game of solitaire. The man clicked his mouse and the screen cleared.

The Election Calculation

"Yes, sir," Stephanie replied. "I was told I could find information on the candidates."

"You can," he said, "but you'll have to give me a little more information. Is this a state or county election?"

"Um, county, I guess. It's for the school board election."

"Yes, that would be county," he said. "What kind of information are you looking for?"

"I'm not really sure," she admitted.

"Well, how about I print out the basic info and you can tell me if that's enough for you?"

Stephanie nodded. The man clicked his mouse a few times, tapped on his computer keyboard, and clicked the mouse again, and the printer behind him began to spit out sheets of paper. When it stopped, he bundled the sheets together and stapled them in the corner.

"Here you go, young lady," he said as he placed the stack of papers on the counter. "Can I ask why you're interested in these candidates?"

"Well, I'm a reporter for our school newspaper and just wanted to be more informed about the upcoming election."

He gave her an appraising look and nodded. "Good for you. We need more people to take a closer look at the candidates they're voting for. I think we'd end up with better elected officials if everyone did that."

Stephanie took the bundle of papers and turned to leave.

"Don't you want to take a look at them before you

go?" he asked. "Feel free to have a seat and scan through them. If there's something else you need, it'll save you a trip back here."

Stephanie thanked him and sat down in one of the hard plastic chairs lining one wall. There was information on each of the six candidates running for the school board, but Stephanie quickly noticed a difference between them. For the ones already on the board—Mr. Bilson, Mr. Santosh, and Mrs. Carmichael—there were three to four sheets of information, including their previous election history and links to their websites and social media. For the new candidates, though, the ones she was most interested in, there was only a single sheet of paper for each with almost no information. She looked carefully at the sheet for Samuel Woodley, the one who had introduced himself at the school board meeting.

Candidate Name: Samuel B. Woodley

Address: 124 Carson Street, Apt 2B, Maynard, VA

Phone:

Time at current residence: 2 months

Occupation: Consultant

Company: Self-employed

Education:

Professional Licenses and Certifications:

Criminal History:

The Election Calculation

The information for Rebecca Tomlin and Thomas Patrick was just as sparse. Stephanie took the packet of papers to the desk.

"Yes?"

"Um, I think I'm missing some information," she said. "There is only one sheet for each of the new candidates."

The man behind the desk tapped on his computer keyboard, scanned the screen, and shook his head. "I'm sorry, but that's all we have."

"Is that unusual?" Stephanie asked.

"Well, the candidates aren't required to provide much info, just what you see. Most, of course, provide quite a bit more. Websites, social media links, voting records, whether or not they have kids in the district, you name it. Whatever they think might get them a vote."

"Okay, thanks," Stephanie said.

She took the bundle of papers outside and took some notes while she waited for her dad. It didn't take her long to spot similarities between the new candidates.

All lived in apartments. Not just that, but in the same building!

All had lived there for only two months.

All were self-employed consultants.

That's too many coincidences, Stephanie thought. *There's got to be some connection.*

A beep woke her from her thoughts. She waved at her dad and jumped into the front seat.

"Find everything you needed?" he asked.

"No," she said, "and that might actually tell me more."

"Less is more?" her dad asked in confusion.

"In this case, it is," Stephanie said without providing further details.

On the way home, she counted fifteen signs advertising the slate of Woodley, Tomlin, and Patrick.

Something is definitely fishy here.

Chapter 10

On Saturday morning, Stephanie had soccer practice with her middle school team. Even though she was younger than many of the girls, she had made the team with ease. The coach had moved her from her normal position of center forward to left winger, but she was quickly adjusting to her new role on the team. She had fewer goals, but a lot more assists. It didn't matter to her as long as the team was winning, and they were undefeated after four games.

She decided to walk to Catherine's house after practice for the math club meeting. It was a couple of miles, but it was a good way to cool down after two hours of running. Also, she knew if she took a slightly different route to her friend's house, she could go past Carson Street. It was a good opportunity for her to continue her investigative reporting.

She used a maps application on her phone to find the best way to get there. After one turn in the wrong direction, she found the street. From there, it was easy to locate the two-story apartment building at 124 Carson Street. Stephanie shuddered as she realized it looked very similar to the building where kidnappers had held Catherine's dad before Stephanie and her friends were able to decipher the message he had sent Catherine. They had recklessly plunged into rescuing him without thinking about their own personal safety. Now Stephanie wondered if she was doing something foolish again.

No, this is different, she thought. *I'm just following up on a story. There could be a perfectly logical reason why three people who just moved into the same apartment building decided to spend thousands of dollars to run for the school board.* She rolled her eyes. *Yeah, and pigs can fly!*

She entered the apartment building through the front door. In the small lobby, there was an elevator, a staircase leading to the second floor, and a long hallway leading to the first-floor apartments. Not much else to see, but then her eyes fell on the row of mailboxes. Each mailbox had the name of the resident on a narrow strip of paper. Stephanie looked and saw the three candidate names. She had come to the right place!

She jumped when the door behind her opened. She spun around in fright but then relaxed. It was just the mailman pulling a wheeled dolly into the building. He used his master key to open the mailboxes. Sorting through the mail, he placed letters, magazines, and advertisements

The Election Calculation

in the appropriate boxes. Stephanie watched closely and noticed the boxes for the three candidates were packed full, making it difficult for the mailman to stuff in the flyer he was putting in each box.

That's strange; they're not picking up their mail.

That thought played in her mind as she walked to Catherine's house from the apartment building. What did it mean that they weren't picking up their mail? Were they not really living there? Why rent an apartment if you weren't going to use it?

As she walked up onto Catherine's front porch, a final thought came to her: she needed to find a way to get a look inside one of those apartments.

"About time you got here," Justin said when Stephanie plopped tiredly onto the couch in Catherine's living room.

"It's been a busy morning," Stephanie replied.

"What's going on?" Catherine whispered to her best friend.

"I'll tell you after the meeting," Stephanie whispered back.

"Okay, Jordan, you called the meeting," Catherine said. "What have you got for us?"

"Elections," he said. "The only way we can get rid of Kenny is to get somebody else elected president of the math club. We've got a few meetings to call for elections, but we can't win unless we come up with a strategy. Now, I've been doing some research on different voting methods."

He opened his notebook and turned to the first page. At the top of the page, he had written *Plurality Voting*.

"First, we have plurality voting. Everybody just votes for one person and the person who gets the most votes wins. You don't even need to get more than half the votes, just more than everybody else. I thought at first that we might be able to run more people and split off some of Kenny's votes, but I don't think that's going to work."

"You're right," Stephanie agreed. "There are sixteen votes and he's pretty much guaranteed to get twelve of them. Even those people who don't like him would be afraid to vote against him."

"If it's a secret ballot, Kenny shouldn't know who voted against him," Catherine countered.

"True," Stephanie admitted, "but I still don't think we'd get enough votes to beat him."

"One hundred percent agree," Jordan said, remembering his conversation with Deiondre during Op Pop. "So that method looks like it won't work."

He flipped to the next page, which had the heading *Approval Voting*.

"Approval voting was designed to avoid electing someone who most of the people oppose. Each person votes for all candidates they approve of, and the candidate with the most votes wins. This is the method they use for both the American Mathematical Society and the Mathematical Association of America. At first, I

The Election Calculation

thought there might be enough people who don't like Kenny, but there might also be people who don't like us, so I don't think that one will work either."

Another page flip revealed a third page entitled *Ranked Voting*.

"This next one is known as ranked voting," Jordan said.

"How's that one work?" Justin asked.

"Everyone ranks the candidates in order of their preference. Then you put the candidates in order based on the number of first-place votes. Then ... it might be easier if I show you an example. Let's say there are three candidates, A, B, and C, and there are seven people voting. Everyone ranks their candidates like this."

He showed how each person voted on the page.

1. A – B – C
2. A – C – B
3. B – A – C
4. C – B – A
5. C – A – B
6. C – A – B
7. C – B – A

"Now we count up all the first-place votes for each candidate."

Jordan tallied the first-place votes and ranked them based on the results.

Round 1
    C – 4
    A – 2
    B – 1

"After the first round of balloting, C had four first-place votes, A has two, and B has one. We throw out candidate B because they came in last place."

"So the person who voted for B doesn't really get a vote in the next round?" Catherine asked.

"No, they do," Jordan explained. "Since their candidate is gone, their second-place vote becomes their first-place vote. Since they voted A as their next candidate, we add a first-place vote to A and tally again."

Round 2
    C – 4
    A – 3

"And then C wins?" Justin asked.

"Right," Jordan said.

"Do you think that would work for the math club vote?" Stephanie asked.

"Unfortunately, no," Jordan answered. "I think we could run multiple people, but they would just keep getting eliminated until only Kenny was left."

He turned to the fourth page in his notebook. Across the top was written *Borda Count*.

The Election Calculation

"After all of that, I finally came up with one possibility," Jordan said. The rest of the Math Kids leaned forward in anticipation. "This voting method is called Borda Count. It was named after a French guy named Jean-Charles de Borda way back in 1781. It's a little like ranked voting because everyone puts the candidates they want in order. But then, instead of just looking at first-place votes, we give a score to every vote. Let me show you. Let's say people voted the same as they did in the last example."

1. A – B – C
2. A – C – B
3. B – A – C
4. C – B – A
5. C – A – B
6. C – A – B
7. C – B – A

"In this method, you get three points for every first-place vote, two for every second-place vote, and one for every third-place vote. It would look like this."

Candidate	Number of 1st place votes (×3)	Number of 2nd place votes (×2)	Number of 3rd place votes (×1)	Total points
A	2	3	2	14
B	1	3	3	12
C	4	1	2	16

"But C still wins, right?" Justin asked.

"Yeah, but look how much closer A got when we voted this way," Stephanie said. "They only needed to change a vote or two and they could have won."

"Exactly!" Jordan said. "I think this one gives us our best chance to figure out a way to win this thing."

"I don't know," Catherine said. "It still looks pretty bad."

"Maybe," Jordan said, "but it at least gives us a chance."

Chapter 11

"Okay, what's going on with your story?" Catherine asked, changing the subject from the math club elections.

Stephanie told them all about her visit to the election office and what she had found when she went by the apartment building.

"I have to find a way to take a look inside those apartments," Stephanie said.

"Are you talking about breaking in?" Catherine asked.

"No, nothing as drastic as that," Stephanie said. "I was thinking maybe I could just have a peek into one of the windows."

"Didn't you say they were on the second floor?" Justin said.

"Yeah, but there are fire escapes at the back of the building," Stephanie answered. "Maybe I could climb up the ladder and take a quick look in a window."

"But what if you get caught?" Catherine asked.

"I guess I would just say I got lost," Stephanie said.

"You got lost climbing up a fire escape?" Jordan asked, raising an eyebrow at his friend. "Yeah, I'm sure they'd buy that story."

Stephanie pondered Jordan's comment. "Maybe I could go at night. If there were no lights in the window, that would probably mean no one was home. I could climb the fire escape, take a quick peek in the window, and be gone before anyone sees me."

"I don't know, Stephanie," Catherine said, concern clear in her voice. "Doing that by yourself sounds pretty risky."

"Who said anything about going alone?" Stephanie smiled. "I was counting on all of you coming with me."

"Why didn't I see that coming?" Jordan asked. "Why are you investigating these candidates in the first place?"

"You've seen their signs all over the place, haven't you?" Stephanie asked.

"Sure, there are probably ten on my street alone," Jordan said.

"Why are so many people putting their signs in their yard?" Stephanie asked.

"I guess they must know them," Justin said.

"That's just it," Stephanie countered. "I don't think they do. From what I found, these three have only lived here for a couple of months. They don't have any kids in the district. They all live in the same apartment building, but it doesn't look like any of them are picking up their mail. Doesn't that seem strange to you?"

The Election Calculation

"I guess, but why are they even running for school board? No one really cares about that anyway," Jordan said.

"That's what I thought," Stephanie answered. "Then my dad told me that the school board controls the budget for the whole school district. We're talking tens of millions of dollars!"

"Are you kidding me?" Justin said. "That's a lot of money."

"And my dad said I should follow the money."

"Follow the money?" Jordan asked. "What's that mean?"

"I asked that same question," Stephanie said. "My dad told me that they wouldn't be running for school board unless there was something in it for them. That's when he said I should follow the money."

"What money?" Catherine asked.

"That's what we need to find out," Stephanie said.

"We? When did *your* news story suddenly become *our* story?" Jordan asked.

"Because we're a team, right?"

Everyone looked around the room. They had been through so much together over the past few years, from standing up to bullies to chasing down burglars to rescuing Catherine's dad from kidnappers to stopping thieves from stealing the Crown Jewels. They couldn't have done any of those things by themselves, only as a team.

Without a word, Justin put his hand forward. Jordan put his hand on top of Justin's. Catherine added hers. With a wide grin, Stephanie put her hand on top of the others.

Justin was the first to break the silence and say what they were all thinking, "Let's do this!"

"Does tonight work for everyone?" Catherine asked.

There were nods all around.

"Okay, let's meet at my house right after dinner," Jordan said. "My mom is cooking pork chops, and I don't want to miss that."

Justin got up from the couch. "I'd better get going then. That doesn't leave me much time to prepare."

"Prepare? What do you need to prepare?" Catherine asked.

"I don't know if you've ever noticed, but our plans don't always turn out quite like we thought," he said. "I like to have some backup plans just in case."

"Okay, eight at Jordan's house it is," Stephanie said. She paused for a moment and looked at each of her friends. "And thanks, guys. I knew I could count on you."

Everyone but Justin was in Jordan's front yard at eight o'clock.

"Where's Justin?" Stephanie asked, tugging at her ponytail.

"He'll be here," Jordan said, looking across the street at his best friend's house in anticipation. "He called a few minutes ago and said he was loading up his backpack."

The Election Calculation

"Oh, no," Catherine said. "That could take forever."

"Nope, here he is now," Jordan said.

Justin came trudging across the street, his ever-present backpack looking even more stuffed than usual.

"What could he possibly be bringing?" Stephanie asked.

"Don't know and didn't bother to ask," Jordan grinned. "But remember, it always seems to have just what we need, doesn't it?"

Stephanie thought back to the tunnel under the Maynard mansion. Justin had packed flashlights, bandanas, spray paint to mark their trail, a ball of yarn that had allowed them to find their way out in the dark, and rope that they'd used to pull Cletus Maynard out of the pit that he fell into. It was like Justin knew exactly what they would need before they even needed it.

"Okay, ready to go?" Justin said when he joined the group.

"We are now," Jordan said. "Let's go."

Stephanie led them to 124 Carson Street. Catherine gasped a little when she saw the building.

"I know," Stephanie said, putting a hand on her friend's shoulder. "It looks like the building where your dad was held."

"It does," Catherine replied, taking a deep breath.

"At least we don't have to rescue anyone this time," Jordan pointed out.

"That's right," Stephanie agreed. "Just a quick peek in the window and we're out of here, I promise."

"Okay, which apartments are theirs?" Jordan asked.

"If the second-floor apartments are numbered the same as those on the first floor, they should be the first three on this end of the building," Stephanie said.

The four friends circled around to the back, keeping close to the building to be less noticeable to anyone on the street. When they reached the back, they looked up at the second floor.

"Good news," Stephanie said. "It looks like all three apartments are dark. That means they're probably not there, just like I suspected."

"And it doesn't look like there are any curtains," Jordan said.

"Um, there's also some bad news," Catherine said. "There's no way to get up to the second floor."

Catherine was right. The lowest rung of each ladder was at least fifteen feet from the ground.

"That doesn't make any sense," Jordan said. "What are you supposed to do? Jump down from the landing? What's the point of the ladders then?"

"I thought there might be this kind of fire escape," Justin said. "They're designed so that the ladders lower to the ground when someone stands on them. That way no one can climb up the ladder and break into someone's apartment."

"Who would do that?" Stephanie asked.

"Um, us," Justin pointed out.

The Election Calculation

"I told you, we're not breaking in. We're just taking a little peek," she protested.

"Okay, then they're made that way so no one can peek into their windows," Justin said.

"That means we're out of luck," Catherine said. "They're too high to reach."

"Not so fast," Justin said as he shrugged his heavy backpack off his shoulders and placed it on the ground. He opened the pack and pulled out a length of rope with something metal on the end of it.

"What is that?" Jordan asked.

"A homemade grappling hook," Justin said proudly. "I made it from some metal coat hangers duct-taped together into hooks."

"What are you going to do with it?"

"If I'm lucky, I'm going to throw it up and catch one of the rungs of the ladder," Justin explained. "Then all we'll have to do is pull the ladder down."

"That's genius!" Jordan said.

"Yeah, it is, if I do say so myself," Justin said.

He unwrapped the rope and swung the grappling hook a few times before launching it. It went about four feet in the air and then fell to the earth. Undaunted, he tried swinging it from a longer length of rope. His second attempt was better, but he was still well short of the ladder.

"I thought it was going to work better than that," he said sadly. "I guess it's not heavy enough."

"It was a nice try, Justin," Catherine said.

Justin shrugged his shoulders. "I wasn't sure if it would work, but I've always wanted to make a grappling hook, so I thought I would give it a shot."

"Maybe we can find some way to make it heavier," Jordan said. "What if we ..."

He stopped when he saw that Justin was pulling more items from his backpack.

"You don't think I came without a backup solution, did you?" Justin asked. He pulled out a plastic gun.

"Is that a gun?" Stephanie asked in alarm.

Justin laughed. "Don't worry, it just shoots plastic darts."

He tied one end of a spool of string onto a dart and loaded it into the gun. Taking careful aim, he shot the dart skyward. It sailed right between two of the rungs on the ladder.

"Nice shot!" Jordan exclaimed.

"Thanks," Justin said.

He carefully let out more string and the dart lowered slowly to the ground.

"Isn't the string going to break if we try to pull the ladder down?" Catherine asked.

"Probably, but we're not going to use the string," Justin said. He tied one end of the string to a length of light rope. He pulled the other end of the string, and the rope was soon looped over the ladder rung. He tugged on the rope and the ladder lowered a few feet toward the ground.

The Election Calculation

"It looks like it's going to work," he said.

"What a great idea," Stephanie said.

"It's not as cool as my grappling hook, but it looks like it'll get the job done."

When the ladder was lowered to the ground, Stephanie took a firm grasp and began to climb.

"Wait a minute!" Justin called out in a loud whisper.

Stephanie looked down. "What is it?" she asked.

"You're going to need this." He handed her a small flashlight.

"I've got a flashlight on my phone," Stephanie said.

"Phone lights are pretty bright," Justin said. "This one also has a red light that's not so noticeable."

Stephanie tucked the flashlight into her pocket and resumed her climb. The others watched as she made her way to the metal landing. From there she could see into two of the apartments. As she stepped off the ladder, it retracted on springs until it was once more unreachable from the ground.

Now, let's see what's going on in these apartments, she thought to herself.

Without using the flashlight, Stephanie peeked around the edge of the apartment window to her left. Seeing no sign of activity, she dared turning on the flashlight, using the red light to make sure no one was in the apartment before turning on the brighter light. She beamed it around what looked like a small living room. It was completely bare, not a couch or a chair to be seen. Shining the light further into the room, she could see through a doorway into what was probably a bedroom, except there was no bed, no dresser, no nightstand. It was another empty room. There was no sign anyone lived in the apartment.

There was a loud creak of metal as she worked her way to the other side of the fire escape. Stephanie was startled and paused for a few moments to let her racing heart settle down again. She looked down and could just make out her friends in the growing darkness. She gave them a thumbs up, took a deep breath, and peered into the second apartment. She was surprised to see that this one wasn't empty. Against one wall, there were stacks and stacks of yard signs. In the center of the room, there was a small card table and a metal folding chair. There was a pizza box on the table with a couple of curled slices of pizza remaining. A half-empty water bottle stood to one side of the table next to a notepad and pen. She tried to make out the writing, but it was too far away to read. She pushed her nose to the glass to try to get closer. That's when she noticed that the window was open. Just a crack, but it was open.

Stephanie slid the window up a few inches, then a few more. When there was enough room, she put one leg through the opening. Bending down, she was able to slide her body through. And before she could think about how foolish her actions were, she was in the apartment!

The Election Calculation

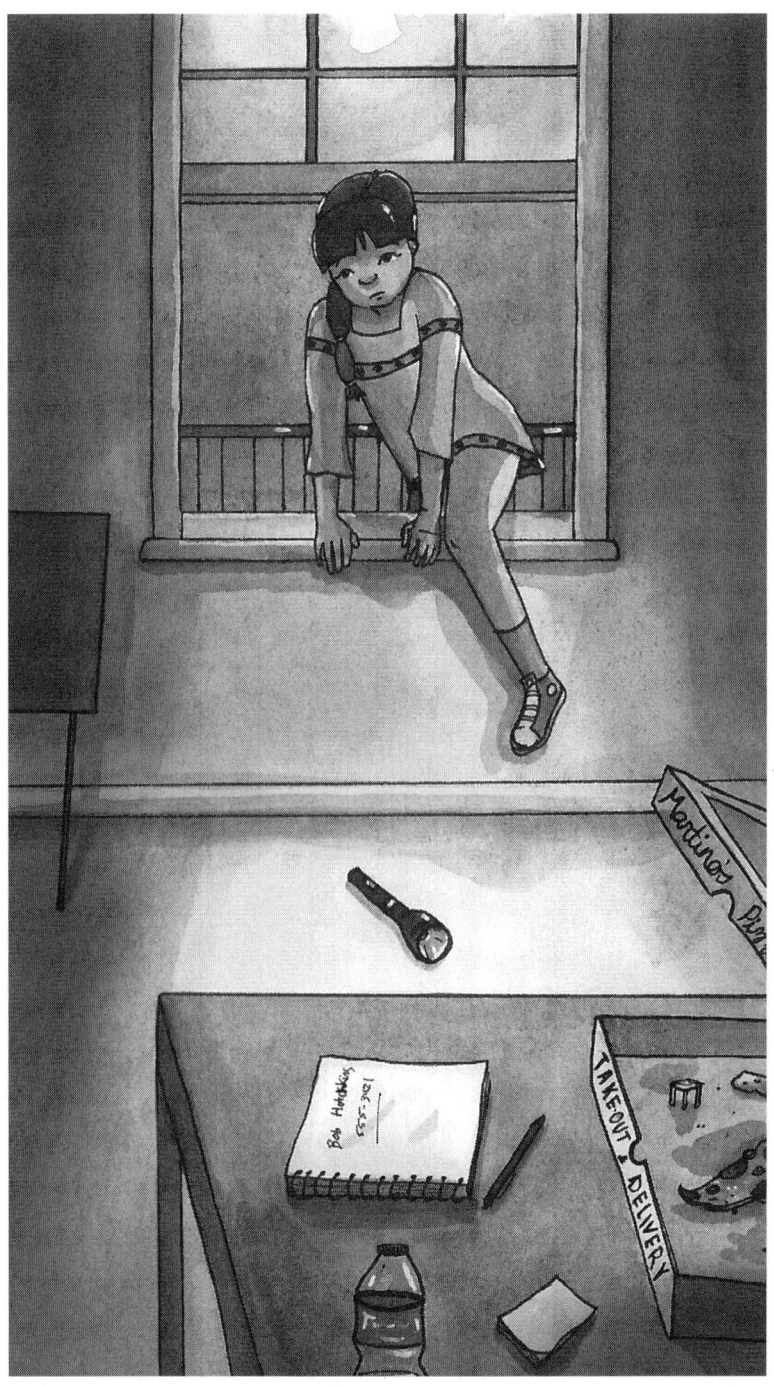

She immediately went to the table and shined the light on the notepad. There wasn't much written, just a name and a phone number.

She used her phone to take a picture of the page and turned to leave. She froze as she heard a loud click. Someone was unlocking the door!

Chapter 12

Stephanie had only a second to think. She glanced at the half-open window, but it was too far away for her to get out of the apartment before the door would open. Instead, she ran into the next room and pressed her back against the wall.

The apartment door opened and light streamed through the doorway as someone turned on a light in the living room. Stephanie looked around her hiding place. It was probably a bedroom, but it was bare of any furniture. No bed to slide under, no dresser to squeeze behind. From the next room, she heard footsteps and some muted mumbling as a man spoke to himself. She slid farther away from the doorway to try to remain out of sight. As she did, her hand brushed against a doorknob. She slowly turned the knob and silently pulled the door open. It was a closet. She eased into the small space and closed the door behind her.

In the darkness, Stephanie could feel her heart pounding in her chest. It seemed loud enough for the man in the next room to hear it, and she took several deep breaths to try to calm down. She was startled by a vibration in her pocket. She reached into her pants to pull out her phone. Looking at the screen, she saw a text message from Catherine: *U OK?*

She texted back: *Man in apt. Hiding in closet*

Catherine's quick reply: *Help coming. Get ready to run!*

Stephanie replied with two emojis:

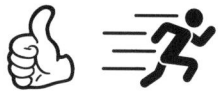

She put her phone back in her pocket and waited, one hand poised near the doorknob so she could quickly throw open the door. She didn't know what her friends had planned, but she wanted to be ready to go when it happened.

Her heart froze in her chest as she heard footsteps approaching. The man had come into the bedroom!

"Now where did I put that stack of brochures?" the man said, now just steps from the closet door. "I must have stuck them in the closet."

Stephanie tensed, getting ready to dash past him as he opened the door. She might not make it, but it would be her only option.

Suddenly, there was loud pounding coming from the other room.

"What now?" the man asked irritably.

The Election Calculation

His footsteps faded as he left the room. Stephanie cracked the closet door open and took a quick peek out. The man was nowhere in sight. She prepared to run for the window as soon as the coast was clear.

"Fire! Fire!" the man shouted from the front door.

Stephanie didn't wait to hear more. She ran for the window. As she crawled through, she looked back over her shoulder. The man was in the doorway of the apartment. A plume of smoke blocked the hallway. Fearing that the man might choose to go out the fire escape, she quickly hopped onto the ladder, which started to slowly descend.

"Hurry!" shouted Catherine from beneath her.

"I'm going as fast as I can," Stephanie replied. When the ladder was close enough to the ground, she leapt off and landed gracefully in a half crouch.

"Let's go!" Catherine said.

The two girls ran around the building. Stephanie saw Jordan and Justin emerging from the front door as she and Catherine rounded the corner of the building.

The four ran toward the street, Justin struggling to keep up due to his shorter legs and the weight of his overstuffed backpack. They heard shouting behind them, but they didn't pause to turn around. They didn't slow until they reached the end of the street and were able to duck out of sight behind a brick wall.

"What was that?" Jordan asked in a gasping breath.

"What was what?" Stephanie asked. She looked at Catherine, but her friend just shrugged her shoulders.

"All that smoke," Jordan said.

Justin grinned but waited to catch his breath before answering.

"A little science experiment," he said in way of explanation.

"A science experiment?" Jordan asked. "You set the apartment on fire!"

Catherine and Stephanie looked on with shocked expressions.

"Did you really start a fire?" Catherine asked.

"It wasn't a fire," Justin said.

"Well, what was it then?" Jordan asked.

"I just dropped some manganese dioxide into a two-liter bottle with a little hydrogen peroxide," Justin explained. "You see, the manganese dioxide acts as a catalyst for the—"

"In English please," Stephanie said.

"I made steam," Justin said.

"A lot of steam," Jordan said.

"Okay, I made a *lot* of steam," Justin agreed.

"And why did you just happen to have magnetic doozy-oxide?"

"Manganese dioxide," Justin corrected.

"Whatever. Why did you have that with you?"

The Election Calculation

"You never know when you're going to need a diversion," Justin said.

"You could have at least warned me," Jordan growled.

"Where's the fun in that?" Justin grinned. "Besides, it worked, didn't it?"

Stephanie laughed. "He's right. Whatever he did got me out of that apartment."

"And what happened to 'I'm just going to peek in the window'?" Catherine said in a serious voice.

Stephanie looked down. "Yeah, about that ..." she said. "You see, I ..." Her voice trailed off as the risk of what she had done finally sunk in.

"You don't know anything about these people," Catherine scolded. "I can't believe you broke into that apartment."

"You're right, Catherine," Stephanie said. "I guess I got caught up in the heat of the moment. I saw some writing on a notepad, and I wanted to see what it said. The next thing I knew, I was in the apartment. I was getting ready to leave but I heard someone unlocking the door and I panicked. I admit it was stupid."

"So stupid," Catherine chastised her.

"Okay, we all get it," Jordan said. "Not her wisest move. But ..."

"But what?" Catherine snapped.

"But what was on the notepad?" Jordan finished.

Stephanie pulled out her phone and pulled up the picture.

"Who's Bob Hotchkins?" Justin asked.

"That's what I need to find out," Stephanie said.

Chapter 13

The Math Kids met at Stephanie's house the next afternoon to work on the problem set from the math club. They breezed through the first eight but got stuck on a logic problem.

"Why can't they just stick to math problems?" Justin complained.

"Because math is based on logic," Catherine said. "If it wasn't for logic, they wouldn't have been able to prove any of the mathematical theorems."

"Well, that doesn't mean I have to like logic problems," Justin grumbled.

"Okay, let's read it again," Stephanie said. "There are three boxes. Each box contains either two white balls, two black balls, or one white and one black ball. Each box is labeled either WW, BB, or BW, but the labels are wrong on each box. Can you determine the contents of all the boxes by drawing just one ball from one box?"

"No," Justin said. "Let's move on to the next problem."

Stephanie glared at him. "Okay, I'll tell Kenny you weren't able to solve it."

"That's not fair," Justin said.

"Like Kenny likes to say, nobody said life is fair," she replied.

"Okay, fine. I'll work on it," Justin said.

> Wait! Do you want to try to solve this problem before the Math Kids?
>
> **There are three boxes, each containing either two white balls, two black balls, or one white and one black ball. Each box has a label of either WW, BB, or BW, but the labels are all wrong. Can you figure out the contents of all the boxes by drawing just one ball from one of the boxes?**

"I guess we should start by drawing out the possible options," Jordan said.

"You think a picture or a table would work better?" Stephanie asked.

"I think a table," Catherine said. "I was thinking something like this."

She drew a table on a sheet of paper.

Incorrect Label	Correct Label	Contents
WW	BW or BB	
BB	WW or BW	
BW	BB or WW	

The Election Calculation

"Does that make sense?" Catherine asked.

"Yep," Jordan said. "So, which box do we draw from?"

"Let's start with box *WW* and see what happens," Catherine said. "If we draw a white ball, we know that box must have one white and one black ball."

"Yeah, but then what?" Justin asked. "We still wouldn't know what's in the other two boxes."

"Maybe we would," Jordan said.

"How?" Justin asked.

"We know all the labels are wrong, right?" Jordan said. "And now we know the box labeled *WW* is really *BW*."

He modified Catherine's table with the new information.

Incorrect Label	Correct Label	Contents
WW	BW or ~~BB~~	BW
BB	WW or BW	
BW	BB or WW	

"And that means the box labeled *BB* can't be *BW*," Jordan continued. "That means it must be *WW*."

"And then the box labeled *BW* must really be *BB* since it can't be *WW*," Stephanie added.

Catherine finished the table.

Incorrect Label	Correct Label	Contents
WW	BW or ~~BB~~	BW
BB	WW or ~~BW~~	WW
BW	BB or ~~WW~~	BB

"Huh, that was easier than I thought," she said.

"Yeah, a little too easy," Justin said.

"What do you mean?"

"What if you drew a black ball out of the box instead?" Justin asked.

Catherine's face fell. "Oh no! If we draw a black ball, we don't know if the box is *BW* or *BB*."

"Exactly," Justin said. "See? This is a stupid problem. Let's just move on to the next one."

"Not so fast," Stephanie said. "What if we pulled from the box labeled *BB* instead?"

"Same problem," Justin said smugly. "It's fine if you pull a black ball, but you won't know anything if you pull a white ball."

Stephanie smiled. "Fine, that means we've found two ways that don't work. Remember that Thomas Edison failed thousands of times before he came up with the light bulb."

Justin scowled and started to say something, but Jordan jumped in instead. "Well, we're down to the last box, *BW*. Let's see if that one works."

"I think it does!" Catherine said. "If we pick a black ball, we know the box is really *BB*. That means the box labeled *WW* must really be *BW* and the box labeled *BB* must really be *WW*."

She drew a new table to show what she was saying.

The Election Calculation

Incorrect Label	Correct Label	Contents
WW	BW ~~or BB~~	BW
BB	WW ~~or BW~~	WW
BW	BB ~~or WW~~	BB

"But what if you draw a white ball?" Justin asked.

"Same logic," Stephanie said triumphantly. "Only now we know the box labeled *BW* is really *WW*. That means the box labeled *BB* is really *BW* and the box labeled *WW* must be *BB*."

She added a table beneath Catherine's latest table.

Incorrect Label	Correct Label	Contents
WW	~~BW or~~ BB	BB
BB	~~WW or~~ BW	BW
BW	~~BB or~~ WW	WW

Everyone looked at Justin. He looked closely at both tables and reluctantly nodded.

"Okay, that looks like it works," he said. "But I still say logic problems are stupid."

"But at least we can show Kenny that we got it," Stephanie countered.

"Yeah, but what does it matter?" Jordan said. "We don't have the votes to take over the presidency, and as long as he is president, there's no way he's going to let us compete."

"Do you think you could convince Trudy to vote against her brother?" Stephanie asked Catherine.

"I doubt it," Catherine said. "She seems pretty loyal to Kenny even though I think she knows he's kind of a jerk."

"Not kind of a jerk," Jordan said. "Kenny is the definition of a jerk. In fact, I bet if you looked up *jerk* in the dictionary, you'd find a picture of Kenny."

Catherine and Stephanie laughed. They looked over at Justin, but he was intently staring at a painting on the wall of Stephanie's living room. He looked like he was in "the zone." Everyone went silent so they wouldn't disturb him. When Justin went into the zone, he tuned out everything around him. You could wave your hands in front of his face, and he might not even notice. But it was what happened when he came out of the zone that mattered. Because he always came up with something amazing.

The three friends watched expectantly for several minutes. Justin just continued to stare. Stephanie looked at the painting she had seen hundreds of times, trying to imagine what Justin was seeing. It was a beautiful portrayal of an English garden, with foxgloves, primroses, sweet peas, bluebells, daisies, towering hollyhocks, and, of course, roses in all colors. Red roses were predominant, but in the center was a single pink rose.

"I think I may have an idea," Justin said, breaking the silence.

The Election Calculation

"What is it?" asked Jordan eagerly.

"The pink rose," Justin replied cryptically, then refused to say anything more.

Chapter 14

The school week passed quickly.

On Monday after school, Justin, Jordan, and Catherine watched Stephanie as she scored two goals in the girls' soccer team's victory over Belmont Middle School. Even Justin, who wasn't usually interested in sports other than basketball, cheered wildly throughout the game.

On Tuesday, Stephanie submitted two story ideas, one on the graffiti recently painted on the wall outside the gym (she suspected a rival school was responsible) and another on the lack of variety on the lunch menu. Neither story was accepted, the first because she had no proof of who had painted the graffiti, and the second because they had run a similar story the previous year. Stephanie was okay with the rejections as it gave her more time to focus on the election story.

Mrs. Bronson asked Stephanie to stay for a moment after the rest of the newspaper staff had left.

"Yes, ma'am?" Stephanie asked.

The Election Calculation

"How's the story on the new candidates coming?" her teacher asked. "You know, the one I didn't give you permission to pursue."

Stephanie smiled. "The story I don't have permission to work on has taken several interesting twists."

Mrs. Bronson raised an eyebrow. "Interesting twists?"

Stephanie nodded.

"And when might I learn more about these twists?" Mrs. Bronson asked. "The election is only two weeks away."

"I know," Stephanie said. "I'm tracking down a good lead that may break the story wide open." She didn't tell her teacher about sneaking into the apartment to look for information on the candidates.

"I look forward to seeing what you're writing on your own time with no approval from me," Mrs. Bronson said with a wink. "Just remember that the clock is ticking."

On Wednesday, Jordan gave his first oral report in his English class. The assignment was to write about what he did over the summer and then give a speech to the class. Jordan described his trip to London and how he and his friends had helped to thwart the theft of the Imperial Crown. The reaction was not what he expected. Most of the class just stared at him in disbelief. Some outright laughed.

"Mrs. Neely, I thought we were supposed to write about what we really did, not some made up stuff," Jeff Branson complained.

"It's not made up!" Jordan protested.

"Right," Jeff said sarcastically. "I'm sure you worked with Scotland Yard and MI7 to save the Crown Jewels."

"It's MI6," Jordan corrected, "and it wasn't all the Crown Jewels, just the Imperial Crown."

"Whatever. You made the whole thing up."

"I did not!"

"Okay, that's enough from the both of you," said Mrs. Neely. "Jordan, I'd like you to stay back for a minute after class."

Jordan nodded glumly while Jeff gloated.

After the bell rang and the room had mostly emptied, Jordan made his way to his teacher's desk.

"The assignment was to write about something you did this summer," she began.

"That's what I did," Jordan said.

"You're telling me that you and your friends helped the British secret service solve a crime?" Mrs. Neely asked. "I hope you understand that your story seems a little farfetched. Are you sure it wasn't the plot of some movie you saw?"

"No," Jordan said defiantly. "It's what really happened. You can ask my friends, and they'll tell you the same thing. We even got to meet the queen and she told us we did 'jolly good work.'"

A few students started to trickle into the classroom. Mrs. Neely gave Jordan a long look.

The Election Calculation

"We'll have to leave this for today because I've got another class coming in," she said, "but we're not done with this conversation."

Jordan started to say more, but she held up a hand to stop him.

"You'd better get to your next class," she said.

Jordan gathered up his papers and stuffed them in his backpack. He ran through the empty hallways but was late for Spanish class again. Señor Hernandez looked at the clock.

"Nueve y ocho," Jordan said without having to be prompted with a question.

"Por favor, verme después de clase," Señor Hernandez said.

"You want to see me after class?" Jordan asked hesitantly.

"Lucky guess," his Spanish teacher told him. "Yes, I'd like to see you after class."

Jordan slumped into his seat as Señor Hernandez returned to his lesson.

That afternoon, the four friends went to math club. Kenny started the meeting by talking about a method for solving problems dealing with proportions. He was only a few minutes into his explanation when Justin raised his hand. Kenny glanced in his direction, scowled, and ignored him. He went back to his explanation without another look at Justin.

"I think Justin may have a question," Mr. Cosgrove interrupted.

"Sorry, I didn't see him over there since he's so short," Kenny said. "Maybe you should stand up next time you have a question."

Buzz and the rest of Kenny's buddies laughed. Instead of getting mad, Justin took Kenny's advice and stood.

"Well, what is it?" Kenny asked. "Was I going too fast in my explanation of proportions? Do you need me to explain it to you?"

"No, I already know how to do what you were explaining," Justin replied.

"Then what's your question?"

"It's not really a question," Justin said.

"What is it then?"

"I'd like to call for an election in two weeks," he said.

"An election for what?" Kenny asked.

"For president of the math club," Justin replied.

There was more laughter, but Kenny flushed in anger.

"You want to elect a new president?" Kenny asked.

"I do, and I would like to nominate Catherine and me as candidates," Justin said.

"Is he allowed to do that?" Kenny asked Mr. Cosgrove.

"He is," the teacher replied.

"Fine, then we'll have elections," Kenny said. "And you can nominate all your friends if you want. It won't change the outcome."

The Election Calculation

"Nope, just Catherine and me," Justin said.

"Even easier," Kenny sneered. "I only have two of you to trounce."

The rest of the math club passed without any further drama as everyone worked through a new set of problems provided by Mr. Cosgrove. As the club time ended, Kenny rose in front of everyone.

"Remember we have an election in two weeks," he said. "And also remember that the president chooses who gets to be in the competition."

He let the implication of those words sink in—either vote for Kenny or risk not being able to compete—before smiling over at Justin and his friends.

"May the best person win," he said smugly.

"Oh, they will," Justin replied confidently.

As Stephanie, Jordan, Justin, and Catherine waited outside the school for Justin's mom to pick them up, Jordan turned to his best friend.

"Do you know what you're doing?"

"I think so," Justin said.

"You *think* so?"

"Well, I still have a few calculations to make, but I think we've got a chance to win."

"But why did you nominate both Catherine and you?"

"Because either of us would lose if we went head-to-head against Kenny."

"But nominating both of us makes it even worse,"

Catherine said. "Even if someone does vote for us, won't that be splitting the vote between you and me?"

"Splitting the vote is just what I'm hoping for," Justin replied. "I was thinking about all the research Jordan did on election methods and I'm going to ask to use the Borda method of voting. We just need to make sure that you are the pink rose in the middle of the garden."

"There you go with the pink rose again," Jordan said. "What does that mean?"

Before Justin could answer, his mom pulled into the parking lot, ending their conversation. Justin kept quiet the whole way home, a far-off look on his face.

Chapter 15

On Saturday morning, the skies opened, and the rain came down in buckets, canceling soccer practice for Stephanie. Normally, she would have been disappointed, but she was happy for the opportunity to pursue her story on the school board. The election was coming up fast, and she needed to figure out who Bob Hotchkins was and what he had to do with the school board election.

She searched the internet for two hours, but none of the hundreds of results seemed to have anything to do with education. Without something more to work on, she felt like she had hit a brick wall.

She reviewed her notes from the school board meetings she had attended to see if they would help. She made a list of topics the board had covered:

- New math curriculum
- Performing arts center
- Dress code
- Upcoming school board elections

She saw a note she had written on the side of her notebook when Samuel Woodley had introduced himself.

Mrs. Guidry seemed happy
Woodley was running.

There were only three spots available on the board and if Woodley and his slate of candidates won, that meant Mr. Bilson, Mr. Santosh, and Mrs. Carmichael, current board members, would be replaced. Why would that make Mrs. Guidry happy? Did she want the three current board members ousted? Then Stephanie remembered that Mrs. Guidry had argued with Mr. Santosh about the cost of something. What was it?

She quickly scanned her notes and it suddenly made sense. The performing arts center! Mr. Santosh had thought it was too expensive, but Mrs. Guidry had disagreed.

"Follow the money," her dad had said. Was there something about the performing arts center that was somehow connected to the elections?

Stephanie went back to her internet search, this time using the key words *Hotchkins* and *construction*. And there it was! Robert Hotchkins was the owner of Hotchkins Construction. Was that the connection?

She carefully read through the web page for Hotchkins Construction. There was a long list of construction projects the company had done, including several office buildings,

The Election Calculation

lots of strip malls, and a minimum-security prison, but there weren't any projects listed for the school district.

On the About page, she read about Robert Hotchkins, the owner of the company. There was a picture of him in dress slacks and a sport coat in front of a construction site, smiling broadly as he shook hands with one of the workers. Something about that toothy grin made Stephanie uncomfortable, but she wasn't exactly sure what. She needed to find out how he might be connected to the school board elections. She was missing something, but what was it? If it was related to finances, she knew just who would have the answer—Mr. Santosh, the school board treasurer.

She examined the printouts from her visit to the election board. She read through the information for Mr. Santosh and was surprised to learn he lived only a few streets away. Stephanie decided to pay him a visit. The rain had stopped, but she had to slosh through numerous puddles of water until she arrived at Mr. Santosh's house. There was a red and blue sign in the front yard which read *Re-elect Santosh for the Maynard School Board* in white letters.

Stephanie rang the doorbell and waited. Mr. Santosh answered the door, wearing a pair of jeans and a sweatshirt. She was surprised at first as she had only seen him in suits on her visits to the school board meetings.

"Yes?" he asked as he stood in the doorway.

"Excuse me for bothering you on a Saturday, Mr. Santosh," Stephanie began, "but I'm a reporter for *Tyler Talk*, our school newspaper, and I was hoping I could ask you a few questions about the upcoming election."

Mr. Santosh smiled. "Certainly, young lady. Come on in."

He stood aside to let her in, but Stephanie looked at her soaked shoes. "How about we talk here on the front porch instead?"

She gestured toward two wooden Adirondack chairs.

"That works for me," Mr. Santosh replied.

Stephanie perched on the edge of one of the chairs and opened her notebook.

"I won't take up much of your time," she said.

"And what was your name again?" he asked.

"Oh, I'm sorry, my name is Stephanie Lewis. This is my first year at Tyler Middle School."

"You look familiar," Mr. Santosh said.

"I just started on the newspaper," she replied, "and I think the new kids always get stuck going to the board meetings." She immediately blushed when she realized what she had said. "I'm sorry, I didn't mean to say 'stuck.' The meetings are actually more interesting than I thought they would be. I mean, it's not that I thought they would be boring. It's just that ..."

Mr. Santosh laughed. "No need to apologize. Just between you and me," he whispered conspiratorially, "the meetings can get a little boring sometimes."

The Election Calculation

Stephanie sighed in relief.

"So, what do you need to know about the upcoming elections?" Mr. Santosh asked.

"My questions are not really about the elections," Stephanie explained.

Mr. Santosh leaned forward. "They aren't?"

"No," she said. "Well, they might be, but I'm not sure. What I'm trying to find out is whether Hotchkins Construction has anything to do with the new performing arts center."

Mr. Santosh raised an eyebrow and gave Stephanie a long look. "Why do you think that?"

"I'm afraid I can't tell you that," Stephanie replied.

"Protecting a source?" he asked.

"No, I just can't tell you where I got the name," she answered.

"Fair enough," Mr. Santosh said. "It's public record anyway, so I can tell you that Hotchkins Construction has submitted a bid to do the construction work on the new performing arts center."

Stephanie's eyes widened. "Who makes the decision on which bid to accept?"

"There is a committee that will review the bids, but ultimately it's the decision of the school board," he said.

"And when will they make the decision?" she asked.

"In about six weeks," Mr. Santosh said.

"So, after the election?" Stephanie asked.

Mr. Santosh nodded.

Stephanie rose from the chair and extended her hand to Mr. Santosh. "Thank you so much for the information."

She started to walk away, then stopped and turned.

"Mr. Santosh?"

"Yes?"

"How much is the new performing arts center going to cost?"

"We won't know until we choose the company," he answered. "We have thirteen million dollars budgeted, but it could go as high as twenty million depending on which contractor we choose."

"There's a big difference between thirteen and twenty million," she said.

"Yes, there is," he replied. "And that explains why this election is so important."

"And maybe it also explains the phone number," Stephanie said to herself.

"The phone number?" Mr. Santosh asked.

"Oh, sorry," Stephanie said. "I'm afraid I can't say anything more right now."

She left Mr. Santosh standing on his porch with a puzzled expression on his face.

Stephanie stopped at the park on the way home. She sat on a damp bench and pulled out her notebook again. She jotted some notes as she tried to put the pieces of the puzzle together.

The Election Calculation

1. Mrs. Guidry and Mr. Santosh disagreed about the performing arts center.
2. Mrs. Guidry seemed happy about the new people running for election.
3. The decision on who does the construction won't come until after the election.
4. There are seven members of the school board, so it would only take four to make the decision. If Mrs. Guidry combined her vote with those of the new candidates (if they get elected), they'd be able to choose Hotchkins Construction for the performing arts center.
5. The new candidates seem to be very well funded. Bob Hotchkin's phone number was found in one of the candidate's apartments. Did he have something to do with funding their campaign?

Stephanie sat back and read through her notes. Was she really saying that Hotchkins was funding the new candidates so he would have enough votes to win the bid for the new construction?

Chapter 16

"Do you think I'm reading too much into this?" Stephanie asked Catherine.

Stephanie had gone straight from the park to Catherine's house and the two were in the basement discussing Stephanie's story, well out of the earshot of Catherine's dad. Catherine read her friend's notes and shook her head.

"No, I think your conclusion makes sense," Catherine said. "I mean, why else would Hotchkins' number have been in that apartment if the two men don't know each other?"

"But does that mean Hotchkins is trying to fix the election?" Stephanie asked. "I mean, maybe they're just friends or work together or something. Maybe there's no connection to the election."

"Then it's up to us to find the connection," Catherine said.

"Yeah, but where do we start?"

"Well, if Hotchkins is funding the candidates, there

must be some records somewhere. I mean, somebody had to pay for all those signs and radio ads, right? Like your dad said, let's follow the money."

"Maybe we could call the radio station," Stephanie said.

"I've got a better idea," Catherine said. "One of our neighbors has one of their signs in their front yard. Maybe we can ask them where they got their sign."

"What if they ask why we want to know?"

"We'll just tell them my dad wants to support the candidate."

"Great idea!" Stephanie said. "Let's go check it out."

Catherine and Stephanie walked down the street to a two-story brick house near the corner. A familiar white sign was in the front yard. It was familiar because they were used to seeing them all over town by now. Blue letters said *Working Together for a Better Education System* with the three candidates' names in bold red letters below.

Catherine was halfway to the front porch to talk to her neighbors when Stephanie called her name from the sidewalk.

Catherine turned around. "What is it?"

Stephanie smiled. "There's no need to find out where they got the sign," she said. "It says it right here."

Catherine returned to the sign and Stephanie pointed out the small print at the bottom: *Canterbury Printing Company.*

"That just says who printed the sign," Catherine said.

"Exactly," Stephanie said. "So that's our next stop. Someone had to pay for the signs. Let's go find out who it was."

Canterbury Printing was way on the other side of town, but Catherine's dad agreed to drive them over.

"Is this for a school project?" he asked as they waited at a stop light.

"It's research for an article I'm writing for the school newspaper," Stephanie said.

"Good for you," Catherine's dad said as he pulled up in front of the building. "Never underestimate the power of the press."

"Thanks, Dad," Catherine said.

"How much time do you need?" he asked.

Catherine looked over at Stephanie. "About twenty minutes should be enough time," she said.

"That sounds about right," Stephanie agreed.

"Okay, I'm going to run a couple of quick errands, and I'll pick you up after that."

"Thanks, Dad," Catherine said as she and Stephanie got out of the car.

"So what do you think we should do?" Stephanie asked as Catherine's dad drove away.

"Leave it to me," Catherine said. "Just play along."

Catherine entered the print shop, followed closely by Stephanie.

The Election Calculation

"You girls need something?" asked a thin guy with a stack of papers in his hand. He frowned. "You're not here selling cookies or anything, are you? Cause we've already—"

"We wanted to check on pricing for some more signs," Catherine interrupted.

The man perked up his ears at the prospect of a sale.

"Signs?" he asked.

"For the school board election," Catherine said.

"That for the Woodley campaign?"

"Yes, the Woodley campaign," Catherine replied.

"Are you his daughter or something?" the guy asked curiously.

"Um, his niece," Catherine answered.

"Give me a second to get the paperwork," he said.

When the man went into a back room, Stephanie grabbed Catherine's arm. "His niece?"

"It was the first thing that came to my mind," Catherine said with a grin.

They didn't have long to wait. The thin man returned from the back room with a sheet of paper in his hand.

"This is the cost for another thousand signs," he said.

"A thousand?" Catherine gasped.

He looked at the sheet and nodded. "That's what the last order was," he said.

"Um, yeah, I guess I need pricing for a thousand," she said.

He made some notes on the order form in a red pen.

"Do you want me to send it to the same address?" he asked.

"Yes, but let me check it to be sure it's right," Catherine said.

The man looked down at the form. "421 Woodside Terrace?" he asked.

"Yep, that's the place," she said.

"Okay, I'll get the pricing sent out right away."

"Thanks," Catherine said.

"No, thank you," he replied.

She and Stephanie quickly left and walked out of sight of the printing shop's front door. Both girls erupted in laughter.

"I can't believe we pulled that off," Catherine said.

"We?" Stephanie asked. "That one was all you. Are you sure you don't want to be an actress someday?"

Catherine beamed. "Maybe after I write a few math books like my dad."

"Now we just need to find out who lives at 421 Woodside Terrace," Stephanie said.

"Do you think it's Hotchkins?" Catherine asked.

"How about we get the guys and take a little trip there tomorrow afternoon and see for ourselves?" Stephanie asked.

Chapter 17

Right after lunch the following afternoon, the four friends met at Justin's house. Since Woodside Terrace was a few miles away, they decided to ride their bikes. Stephanie took the lead and the other three followed as she pedaled through the rolling hills on the outskirts of Maynard. It was a beautiful fall day that was perfect for a leisurely bike ride, but Stephanie wasn't thinking about that. Her attention was on their destination and hopefully fitting the final piece of the election puzzle into place.

"If I'm right about Hotchkins living there, we know who's been funding the campaign. If he gets his candidates elected, he'll have enough votes to win the bid for the performing arts center."

"That has to be illegal, doesn't it?"

"I don't know, but even if it isn't, we still need to let people know about it," Stephanie said firmly. "And my story is going to do just that."

They crested a hill and looked down on a neighborhood full of large houses circling a small lake with a fountain at its center. The conclave of houses was surrounded by stands of birch trees, their yellow bark standing out in contrast to the immaculate green lawns. Stephanie pulled her bike to the shoulder and stopped so the others could catch up.

"Wow!" Justin said. "So this is where the rich people live."

"Well, if you got your own school board elected and got them to choose your overpriced bid, you could live in a mansion too," Stephanie said.

"What's the plan, Stephanie?" Jordan asked. "Are you just going to knock on the front door and see if this Hotchkins guy lives there?"

"I'm hoping that his mailbox will have his name on it and that will be all the proof we need," Stephanie said.

"Well, let's get riding," Justin said as he swung his short leg back over his bike.

Stephanie nodded and mounted her own bicycle.

The four flew down the hill and only stopped when they got to the sturdy metal fence barring entrance to the neighborhood. Near the gate was a keycard reader.

"Now what?" Catherine asked.

"You don't happen to have a keycard in your backpack, do you?" Jordan asked as he looked over at Justin.

Justin shrugged his shoulders. "Sorry, I'm fresh out."

Catherine looked at the stretch of fence heading off in both directions as far as she could see. "We can't go

The Election Calculation

through it, and it looks like the fence circles the entire neighborhood, so we can't go around it."

"Do you think we can climb over?" Justin asked.

"With those spikes on top?" Stephanie said, pointing to the top of the fence.

"I can't believe we rode all this way for nothing," Stephanie said in frustration.

Jordan smiled. "Oh, I don't think it was for nothing."

"Yeah?" Justin said. "You've got some way to get over that fence?"

"Nope."

"Then what's your plan?" Justin asked.

"Remember that song we used to sing in kindergarten?" Jordan asked. "You know, the one about going on a bear hunt?"

"Yeah, what about it?" Justin asked.

"Well," Jordan smiled. "We can't go through it, can't go around it, can't go over it. That only leaves going under it." He pointed toward a stand of birch trees. "It looks like there is some kind of culvert over by those trees."

"Let's go!" Stephanie said.

She dropped her bike at the fence and peered into a corrugated metal pipe running underneath the fence.

"What do you think it's for?" Catherine asked.

"Probably for stormwater runoff," Jordan said.

"Do you think we can fit through there?" Justin asked doubtfully.

Jordan bent down and peered through the pipe. "It'll be tight," he said, but it looks like it's only about ten feet. I think we can make it."

Before anyone could talk her out of it, Stephanie dropped to her stomach and began to belly crawl through the pipe. Fifteen seconds later, her head emerged from the other side.

"It's a little wet, but it's not too bad," she said as she rose to her feet, wiping damp leaves off of her hands. "Who's next?"

"I'll go," Catherine said, and quickly crawled into the pipe, joining Stephanie on the other side a short time later.

Justin was still looking doubtfully at the pipe. "I don't know, guys," he said. "I'd hate to get stuck in there."

"That's okay," Stephanie said from the other side of the fence. "Catherine and I will go check out the house while you and Jordan stay with the bikes."

Stephanie and Catherine made their way through the woods and onto the road. It didn't take long for them to find 421 Woodside Terrace. It was an imposing house set back from the street with a circle drive in front. A black wrought iron fence surrounded the property. Two large planters stood on either side of a set of stone stairs leading to the front door.

"Wow, look at that place," Catherine said. "Hotchkins must be a gazillionaire if needs another fence inside of a gated community."

The Election Calculation

"Well, he sure didn't spend his money on fancy cars," Stephanie said. She pointed at the two cars parked in the circle drive. One was an old Ford sedan and the other a late model pickup truck that was dented in several places.

"They might not be his," Catherine pointed out. "Maybe he has visitors."

Stephanie wasn't interested in Hotchkins' visitors. "Let's see if we can get a look at the mailbox," she said. "All I want to do is get a picture showing that it's his house."

Catherine walked toward the brick mailbox at the end of the driveway. She looked startled as she got closer.

"What is it?" Stephanie asked.

"I think there's a problem with your assumption," Catherine said.

"Is there a name?"

"Yeah, but I think you need to take a look at this."

Stephanie quickly joined her friend and looked at the mailbox. There was a name, but it wasn't Hotchkins.

The name on the mailbox was Guidry!

"What?" Stephanie exclaimed. "But that can't be right!"

"Mrs. Guidry is funding the election for the new candidates?" Catherine asked. "But why?"

"I have no idea," Stephanie admitted. "I was sure it was Hotchkins. I mean, he stands to gain the most if he can get the school board to choose his bid for the new construction. I can't believe I got it all wrong."

"Maybe you didn't," Catherine said. "Take a closer look at the pickup truck."

Even at a distance, Stephanie could easily read the words on the side of the truck: *Hotchkins Construction*. So Hotchkins was somehow involved!

As they looked toward the house, the front door swung open, revealing Mrs. Guidry and two other men.

"It's Guidry!" Catherine said in a loud whisper.

"And that's not all!" Stephanie said. She recognized Bob Hotchkins from his company's website. And right behind him was Samuel Woodley!

She pulled out her phone and clicked the camera icon. She stuck her phone through the bars of the fence and, zooming in on the three people standing on the front steps of Guidry's house, snapped a picture.

The Election Calculation

"Hey! What are you doing?" Hotchkins yelled as he saw Stephanie with her cell phone.

"I think it's time to go," Catherine said.

"It's past time," Stephanie agreed as she saw Hotchkins and Woodley start to run toward the fence.

The two girls ran as fast as they could away from the house.

"Open the gate!" Hotchkins yelled to Mrs. Guidry as he gave up his chase on foot and headed back toward his truck.

Mrs. Guidry stepped inside the house and the gate began to slowly open while Hotchkins revved his truck engine. Woodley jumped into his car and started it, a plume of black exhaust spewing from the tailpipe.

Both men drove down the driveway and made sliding turns into the road in pursuit of the two girls.

Catherine, looking back at the two vehicles approaching, called out a warning to her friend. "Let's get to the pipe!"

Stephanie made a sharp left into the grass and headed toward the woods, with Catherine right behind her. They had just reached the trees when the two men skidded to a stop.

Hotchkins jumped out of his truck and ran toward the woods. Stephanie and Catherine gained some space as the man tripped on an exposed root and fell heavily to the ground.

"Keep going! We're almost there!" Stephanie yelled.

"Stephanie!" Catherine called out in a panicked voice.

Stephanie looked back and saw that Catherine's sleeve was snagged on a tree branch. Hotchkins had regained his footing and was closing in on her. Stephanie reversed direction to help her friend. She was able to free Catherine, but now Hotchkins was only steps behind. Stephanie grabbed Catherine's hand and pulled her down a slight incline. The pipe was just a few yards in front of them. Jordan and Justin were on the other side of the fence shouting at them to hurry. Stephanie dropped to the ground and crawled through. Jordan helped her to her feet. Catherine entered the pipe and was just seconds from safety when she felt a strong hand wrap around her ankle. She reached out for Stephanie's hand on the other end of the pipe, but she was jerked backward.

"Not so fast, girl," Hotchkins hissed. He yanked Catherine out of the culvert.

"Let her go!" Stephanie yelled.

"Who are you?" Hotchkins asked as he roughly pulled Catherine to her feet.

"Us? We're just kids," Catherine stammered.

"What are you doing taking pictures of us?" Hotchkins demanded.

"Um, we were just taking pictures of the houses in the neighborhood," Stephanie improvised.

"Gimme your phone!" Hotchkins demanded.

"Let go of my friend first," Stephanie said.

The Election Calculation

"Phone first," Hotchkins said, tightening his grip on Catherine's arm. She cried out in pain.

"Fine!" Stephanie said. She approached the fence with her phone. Hotchkins reached through the bars and yanked it out of her hand. Once he had the phone, he shoved Catherine to the ground. Catherine quickly crawled through the pipe while she had the chance.

Hotchkins looked at the front of Stephanie's phone. "What's the password?" he asked.

"What makes you think she's going to give it to you?" asked Justin.

"Well, it's that or I just smash it on this metal pipe," Hotchkins said. "Either way, the picture is history. So, what's it going to be?"

"The password is the first six digits of pi," Stephanie said.

"What?" Woodley asked.

"Three, one, four, one, five, nine," the kids said in unison.

Woodley clicked a few times on the phone and then tossed it to the ground. "The picture's deleted. Now, you kids better stay away from us!" he spat out before turning and tromping back through the woods.

"Are you okay, Catherine?" Stephanie asked anxiously.

"Yeah, I'm fine," Catherine said.

"All that work to get the picture and now it's gone," Jordan said.

"Oh, the picture's not gone," Stephanie said calmly.

"Wait! What? But how?" Catherine said.

"I texted it to Justin before I handed Hotchkins my phone," she explained.

Justin pulled his phone out of his backpack and found Stephanie's text. "It's a great picture," Justin said. "It will be a perfect addition to your story."

"Speaking of which, we'd better get going," Stephanie said. "We file our stories on Tuesday, so that doesn't give me much time."

"Aren't you forgetting something?" Catherine asked. On Stephanie's puzzled look, Catherine pointed at her phone on the other side of the fence.

"Okay, a couple more trips through the pipe and then we'll get going," Stephanie said.

Chapter 18

Stephanie worked furiously on her newspaper article over the next two days. Every free moment she had, she was writing, editing, and double-checking every fact against the information in her notebook. She finally finished the article during study hall on Tuesday afternoon. She printed out a copy and read it through one more time before turning it in. She was thrilled with the result.

The story detailed the attempt to gain control of the school board by having the school board vice president actively working to oust three current members. It told how Stephanie had visited the election board and found out the three new members had all recently leased apartments in the same building. The article laid out how Mrs. Guidry was funding the election and that Hotchkins Construction stood to gain if she was able to get enough votes to choose their bid for the new performing arts center. As proof, there was photographic evidence of Hotchkins, Guidry, and Woodley meeting together. The story had everything, even the personal aspect of Hotchkins chasing her and Catherine through the woods. Stephanie was certain that Mrs. Bronson was going to love it!

Stephanie waited nervously while her English teacher read through the article. She cringed every time Mrs. Bronson frowned and jotted something down on the paper using her red pen. Finally, the teacher placed the paper on her desk and looked up at Stephanie.

"This is really good work," she said with a smile. Stephanie let out a sigh of relief.

"But ..."

Stephanie's heart fell into the pit of her stomach.

"But you need to do a few things to finish the story," Mrs. Bronson finished.

"Like what?" Stephanie asked.

"I don't see a comment from Mrs. Guidry," Mrs. Bronson replied. "What does she stand to gain if they go with Hotchkins for the performing arts center?"

"I don't know," Stephanie admitted. "Maybe Hotchkins promised her a cut of the money?"

"'Maybe' isn't a word journalists like to use in a story," Mrs. Bronson said with a frown. "If you're going to write a story, particularly one that alleges someone is doing something wrong, it's only fair that you allow them to comment on the story before you print it."

"But she'll just deny everything," Stephanie said.

The Election Calculation

"I would expect she will, but you still have to give her a chance to explain her side of the story."

"So do I just go up to her and ask her for a comment?"

"Yes," Mrs. Bronson said. "Without giving her a chance to comment, I'm afraid we can't run the story."

"But the election is next week!" Stephanie protested. "That doesn't give me much time."

"There's a board meeting tonight. Maybe you can get her to comment on the record there."

Stephanie nodded and walked glumly out of the room.

***

"You have to get a comment from her?" Catherine asked in amazement as she and Stephanie walked home from school later that day.

"That's what Mrs. Bronson said."

"But she's just going to lie," Catherine said.

"I know that, and you know that, and I think Mrs. Bronson knows that, but she says we can't run the story without asking her for a comment."

"What are you going to do?" Catherine asked.

"I guess I'm going to the board meeting tonight to ask for a comment."

"I'll go with you," Catherine said.

"Thanks," Stephanie said. "You're a good friend."

Catherine grasped her friend's hand and gave it a squeeze. Stephanie smiled gratefully.

Chapter 19

"How do I look?" Stephanie asked when she opened the door to greet Catherine that evening. She was wearing a blue plaid skirt with a white blouse. In one hand she held a copy of her story and in the other a notepad.

"Like a reporter ready to go into battle," Catherine said.

"That's what this feels like," Stephanie said.

Stephanie's dad drove them to the administration building and dropped them off at the curb. "Are you sure you don't want me to come in with you, Steph?"

Stephanie shook her head. "No, Dad. I've got this."

"Remember," he said, "you never have to be afraid to do what's right."

"Thanks, Dad. I'll see you after the meeting."

Stephanie took a deep breath, clutched Catherine's hand, and walked into the board meeting. She was already tense, but to make matters worse, Mr. Bilson, the board president, wasn't at the meeting. That meant Mrs. Guidry was in charge.

The Election Calculation

Stephanie fidgeted nervously through the board meeting, just waiting for her chance to speak during the public comments. But when it was time for speakers to approach the microphone, she froze. Catherine lightly elbowed her, but Stephanie couldn't get up the courage to rise. She could feel Mrs. Guidry's eyes staring at her.

A few people spoke, but then the small line was gone. There was no one at the microphone. Still, she remained in her seat. Mrs. Guidry looked over the audience and said, "If there is nobody else, we'll close the public comments."

Catherine leaned over and whispered, "The score is tied. You've got the ball, just one person between you and the goal. Are you going to pass or are you going to take your shot?"

Stephanie smiled at the soccer reference. She rose and said in a loud voice, "I'd like to speak."

Mrs. Guidry stared daggers at her. That look was almost enough to buckle Stephanie's already wobbly legs.

"I'm sorry, but we've already closed the open discussion," Mrs. Guidry said, her smile as cold as a winter ice storm.

Stephanie faltered, her approach to the microphone halted mid-step. Then Mr. Santosh came to her rescue.

"I think we have time for one more speaker, don't we?" he asked.

"I closed the public comments," Mrs. Guidry replied sharply.

"I understand, but shouldn't we always take the

opportunity to hear from our students?" Mr. Santosh said. Without waiting for a response, he gave Stephanie an encouraging smile. "Now, young lady, what would you like to discuss tonight?"

Mrs. Guidry started to speak, then pursed her lips tightly together instead.

Stephanie stepped in front of the microphone.

"Mrs. Guidry, my name is Stephanie Lewis. I am a reporter for *Tyler Talk*, the middle school newspaper. I have submitted a story for this week's edition." She paused and took a deep swallow. "It concerns the upcoming school board elections and possible interference from a company that wants to get favorable board consideration for their construction bid."

"I'm sorry, the board can't comment on closed bids," Mrs. Guidry said.

"I'm not asking about the bids, but for a comment on the story itself," Stephanie said.

"And why would the board comment on a middle school story?" the board vice president asked icily.

"Not the board, Mrs. Guidry," Stephanie said. "I'm looking for a comment from you personally."

"Me?" Mrs. Guidry feigned surprise. "Why would I have a comment?"

"Because my research shows that you paid for the signs for the new candidates," Stephanie said. Behind her, the crowd stirred. This was getting interesting. Stephanie

The Election Calculation

walked to the front of the room and laid a copy of the article on the table in front of Mrs. Guidry. "Can you tell us why you are funding these candidates?"

"I have nothing to say to an impudent middle schooler," Mrs. Guidry said sharply.

"Can I put 'no comment' in the article then?" Stephanie asked.

Mrs. Guidry ignored Stephanie's question. Instead, she rose in her chair and said loudly, "If there are no further public comments, I'll consider this meeting adjourned."

Without another word she walked quickly out of a side exit.

"Sounds like a 'no comment' to me," Catherine said loudly. Several people around her laughed.

"That's how it's going in the story," Stephanie agreed. "Let's go. I'm on a deadline."

As soon as she got home, Stephanie added another paragraph to the story detailing the school board meeting and Mrs. Guidry's refusal to read the article and provide a comment. After one final read-through, she emailed the story to Mrs. Bronson.

As she lay in bed, sleep eluded her even though she was exhausted by everything that had happened over the past few weeks. She finally fell into a fitful sleep, where she dreamed about Hotchkins chasing her through a tunnel that got smaller and smaller until there was nowhere left to run.

The Election Calculation

***

Kenny glared at Stephanie and her friends the next day as they walked into the math club room. Buzz said something under his breath to Mike and Phil, two of the boys from the A team. She didn't hear all of it, but she caught the words *losers* and *election*. Whatever it was, Mike and Phil thought it was hilarious.

When Kenny asked if there were any questions about the problem set from the previous week, Justin's hand shot up.

"I should have known you wouldn't have been able to work them," Buzz said. More laughter from Mike and Phil.

"It's not that," Justin replied. "The problems were pretty easy."

"Then what is it?" Kenny asked.

"I'd like to propose we use the Borda Count method for the election next week," Justin said.

"The what?" Kenny asked.

"The Borda Count method," Justin asked. "Everyone orders the people who are running. For example, let's just say you think I'm the only good candidate—"

This was met by a small chorus of boos from Buzz and some of his friends.

"—then you would only vote for me," Justin continued. "But if you wanted Kenny to win and Catherine as your second choice, then maybe you would order us Kenny,

Catherine, and then me. Each candidate gets three points for every first-place vote, two for every second-place vote, and one for every third-place vote."

"Why can't we just vote normally?" Kenny asked.

"What, are you worried you might lose using this method?" Justin asked.

Kenny's face turned red. "Look, we can vote any way you want. I'll win anyway and you and your friends still won't be able to compete."

Chapter 20

Stephanie couldn't wait to get to school on Friday morning. The latest edition of *Tyler Talk* would be out, and she was anxious to see how her story looked in print. The papers were in a rack just inside the entrance. She grabbed a copy, then took three more to share with her friends. She stood to one side of the lobby to read the paper.

Her story wasn't on page one, which was a little surprising considering how important it was. When it also wasn't on page two or three, she began to get concerned. It was a late-breaking story, but she was certain Mrs. Bronson had been saving room for it. But as she flipped page after page, she learned the hard truth. It wasn't there. Her article hadn't made this edition, which means it would be scrapped completely because the elections would be over before anyone could read it. She dropped all four copies of the paper into the recycling bin.

Stephanie had English for second period, and Mrs. Bronson caught her as soon as she walked into class.

"I'm sure you already know ..." Mrs. Bronson began.

"Yeah, I saw the paper," Stephanie said. "I don't know what happened. I got Mrs. Guidry's 'no comment' just like you asked me to do."

"I know."

"Then why did you kill the story?" Stephanie asked, trying desperately not to cry in frustration.

"I didn't."

"Then who did?"

"Mrs. Guidry called me Tuesday night after the board meeting and said she would not allow the story," Mrs. Bronson explained.

"Can she do that? What about freedom of the press and all that?" Stephanie asked.

"That doesn't always apply to school newspapers, unfortunately," her teacher explained. "The courts have said that school officials, in this case the vice president of the school board, can censor certain articles in a school newspaper. Mrs. Guidry decided to do just that."

"It's not fair," Stephanie said. "I worked so hard on that article."

"I know you did," Mrs. Bronson said, "and it was a good article. Not just good, but important. I'm sorry I couldn't do more."

"It wasn't your fault," Stephanie said. "It was Mrs. Guidry, and now she and her friends are going to get away with it."

The Election Calculation

***

At lunchtime, the Math Kids found a table near the back of the school cafeteria.

"I'm sorry you didn't get your story in the paper," Catherine said.

"It was a great article," Jordan said. "And at least our parents won't be voting for those new people and they're spreading the word, so you accomplished something anyway."

"Unfortunately, it probably won't be enough," Stephanie said. "Word of mouth is great, but it's hard to compete with thousands of signs and radio commercials."

"It's not just radio," Justin said. "There was a television ad on last night during the basketball game."

"You're kidding me!" Jordan said.

"I bet they stand to make a ton of money by overbidding on the performing arts center, so they can afford it," Catherine said.

"It just shows you that money can buy elections," Justin said.

"Not just money," Catherine said, "Kenny is using power and intimidation to win the math club election."

"I know," Stephanie agreed. "I just wish there was a way to level the playing field for people who don't have either money or influence. Maybe we'd end up with some better candidates."

Stephanie thought about the upcoming elections over the weekend, especially the unfairness present in both. She felt an overwhelming sense of hopelessness. They were working hard to find enough votes to win the math club election, but she knew in her heart that the numbers just weren't there. And despite her efforts and everything she had risked researching the school board election, her story had been squashed with a simple phone call from Mrs. Guidry.

On Monday morning, Stephanie got dressed and went down to breakfast. Where she normally sat at the table, there was a flat box with a pink ribbon tied around it.

"What's this?" she asked.

Her dad shrugged his shoulders. "I guess you'll have to open it to find out."

"But where did it come from?"

"It was on the front porch when I went out to get the paper," he said.

She unwrapped the ribbon and set it aside. She opened the lid of the box and saw a copy of *The Maynard Gazette*.

"A newspaper?" she asked.

"Read the headline," her dad said.

Stephanie read it and gasped. In bold print, the banner of the paper read:

The Election Calculation

School Board Vice President Under Investigation for Election Fraud

Stephanie read the first paragraph.

> Election officials are investigating suspicious circumstances around the Maynard School Board elections to be held tomorrow. Investigative reporters have found strong ties between Betty Guidry, the current board vice president and three of the candidates running for the school board: Samuel Woodley, Rebecca Tomlin, and Thomas Patrick. In addition, Guidry has been linked to Robert Hotchkins, the owner of Hotchkins Construction. During questioning by officials, Rebecca Tomlin admitted she was hired by Guidry to run for the school board to give preferential treatment to Hotchkins Construction in its bid for the new performing arts center.

There was more to the story, including the picture of Guidry, Hotchkins, and Woodley that Stephanie had taken, but her dad was pointing at the top of the article.

"Did you see the byline?" he asked.

And there it was. The byline credited investigative reporters Stephanie Lewis and Bill Blankenship. The paper was calling her an investigative reporter!

"There's a note too," her dad said, handing her a card.

Stephanie opened the card to find a handwritten note from Bill Blankenship.

> *Thanks for the great work on this story, Stephanie. You're going to be a great reporter—in fact, you already are! I wouldn't have had anything to go on if you hadn't left your story on the table at the board meeting. I spoke to your teacher, Mrs. Bronson, and she told me Guidry squashed your story in your school newspaper, so I didn't think you would mind seeing it in* The Maynard Gazette. *Don't worry about those three getting elected—they may have lots of signs, but the newspaper is still read by thousands of people. Just know that you really made a difference.*
>
> Best,
>
> Bill Blankenship

"Wow!" was all Stephanie could say.

"Wow is right," her dad said. He draped an arm over Stephanie's shoulders. "I'm proud of you. You'll have to tell your mom and me all about your investigation tonight at dinner."

Stephanie figured she had the rest of the day to come up with a version of the story that conveniently left out

The Election Calculation

her visit to Woodley's apartment. In the meantime, she settled back in her chair with a big smile on her face and read the whole article.

Chapter 21

On Wednesday, Stephanie was greeted with high fives from everyone when she entered the school building. The school board election results were in, and Woodley, Tomlin, and Patrick had been trounced following the article in *The Maynard Gazette*. Stephanie had even been interviewed for a story by the local TV station.

"Can I get your autograph?" Justin asked as he held out a copy of the paper.

Stephanie grinned and signed her name under her byline.

"Great work on the school board election," Catherine said. "It's all people are talking about."

She and Stephanie continued to talk as they walked away, leaving Jordan and Justin behind.

"I'm glad Stephanie was able to make a difference in the school board election," Jordan said, "but I'm afraid the math club election isn't going to go as well."

"Have a little faith," Justin said. "I told you I have a plan."

The Election Calculation

"Do you think it's going to work?" Jordan asked.

"It has to," Justin said, "since I don't have a backup plan."

"That's not very encouraging," Jordan replied.

"I've been running numbers all week," Justin said. "We just have to hope everything works out like I've planned it."

"And what if it doesn't?"

"Don't my plans always work?" Justin asked.

Jordan gave his friend a long look. "Do I have to remind you about the time you thought you could win the Cub Scout Pinewood Derby race by taping a bottle rocket to your car?"

"Wait a minute," Justin protested. "That was a great plan. My car was way ahead of the others."

"Until it blew up," Jordan reminded him.

"A minor setback."

"And set the track on fire," Jordan continued.

"Yeah, that was a little unfortunate," Justin conceded.

"A little unfortunate? You were kicked out of the pack," Jordan said.

"Okay, but that's just one example. I'll admit my plans don't *always* work, but don't they *usually* work?"

Jordan thought for a moment. "I'll give you that. Your plans *usually* work. But what if this one doesn't?"

Justin shrugged his shoulders. "Then I guess we'll have some free time when the competition comes around."

"Great," Jordan said, his voice dripping with sarcasm.

Jordan didn't see Justin again until it was time for math club. When he got to the club room, Justin was pacing back and forth, his forehead furrowed as he intently studied his notebook.

"Uh oh," Jordan said.

"Uh oh, what?" Justin said without looking up.

"You look worried."

"Nah, this is just my game face. I think we've got this," Justin said.

"Well, try not to look so worried," Jordan said. "Here come the girls."

Stephanie and Catherine joined them outside the room.

"Well?" Catherine asked.

"All good," Justin said.

"Are you sure?" Stephanie asked.

"As sure as I can be," Justin answered. "We just have to remember one thing when we're voting."

"What is it?" Catherine asked.

Just as Justin began to explain, Buzz came walking down the hall. Justin quickly jotted a few words in his notebook and passed it around to his friends. Stephanie read the note and looked up with a puzzled look on her face.

"Trust me," was all Justin said before closing his notebook and walking into the room.

The Election Calculation

After everyone had settled down, Mr. Cosgrove stood in front of the classroom and looked out at the students in the math club.

"We're going to get started today by holding the election for the next president of the math club," he said. "Remember, as agreed upon by the candidates, we'll be using the Borda Count method to vote. You will list one to three candidates in your order of preference. The candidate listed first will get three points, the candidate listed second will get two points, and the candidate listed third will get one point. When everyone has voted, we'll total up the scores and determine the winner. Everyone understand?"

There were nods around the room. While Mr. Cosgrove wasn't looking, Kenny looked over at Jordan and mouthed "you're going down."

"Okay, I'm going to hand each of you a piece of paper. You'll list your preferences and return the paper to my desk for counting."

He quickly distributed blank sheets of paper. It didn't take long for people to make their choices, and one by one they returned the ballots to Mr. Cosgrove. Justin and his friends looked on nervously while the teacher tabulated the votes. Finally, Mr. Cosgrove looked up from his tabulations.

"I'm done with the calculations and I'm ready to announce the winner," he said.

Kenny rose from his seat. "I am pleased to remain your president," he said with a dramatic bow to his friends. The classroom erupted in applause and laughter. Catherine noted that Trudy did not join in the fun, but instead frowned at her brother and shook her head.

"Please return to your seat, Kenny," Mr. Cosgrove said.

He went to the whiteboard at the front of the room. He drew a table with the candidates and the number of first-, second-, and third-place votes they had received.

Candidate	First	Second	Third	Total Points
Kenny	11	1	0	
Catherine	5	11	0	
Justin	0	0	12	

"Nice scores, Justin," Buzz called out. "Even your friends didn't vote for you."

Most of the class laughed, but Kenny was studying the vote results on the board. "Wait a minute," he said. "Who didn't vote for me?"

There was silence in the room. Kenny turned and looked at his sister Trudy. "It was you, wasn't it?"

Trudy met his stare and nodded.

"Why?" he asked.

"First of all, I don't think it's fair that not everyone gets a chance to be on the A team," Trudy began.

"You're just mad because you're not as good at math as I am," Kenny responded.

The Election Calculation

"But mostly, I'm tired of you acting like a jerk all the time," Trudy finished.

"I'm telling Mom," he said.

Justin snorted out a laugh and Kenny spun in his direction. He pointed at Justin and spit out a response, "You and your friends will never see a competition!"

Justin looked at him and said, "It's not your choice, Kenny."

"What do you mean?"

"Do the math," Justin said with a smile and pointed at the board, where Mr. Cosgrove was adding the totals to the table.

Candidate	First	Second	Third	Total Points
Kenny	11	1	0	35
Catherine	5	11	0	37
Justin	0	0	12	12

"That can't be right!" Kenny yelled. "I got eleven first-place votes. How can I not be the winner?"

Mr. Cosgrove explained, "You got thirty-three points for your first-place votes and two for your second-place vote. That's a total of thirty-five. Catherine got fifteen points for her first-place votes and another twenty-two points for her second-place votes. That's thirty-seven. That makes Catherine the new president."

This time it was the Math Kids who applauded.

But Kenny wasn't done yet. "You didn't add it up right," he protested.

Mr. Cosgrove raised an eyebrow. "Where did I get it wrong?" he asked.

"There are sixteen first-place votes but only twelve second- and third-place votes," Kenny said with a note of triumph in his voice. "You missed some votes."

"No, I didn't," the teacher replied. "There were four ballots with just Catherine's name on it."

"But that's not fair!" Buzz blurted out.

"Actually, it is," Justin said. "It's called bullet voting, where you only vote for a single candidate in a ranked system."

Buzz looked at Justin like he had just spoken in a foreign language. "What?"

"The four of us only voted for Catherine," he explained.

"Is that allowed?" Kenny asked Mr. Cosgrove.

"I said you could list from *one to three* candidates," he replied, taking a glance over at Justin, who shrugged his shoulders in acknowledgment. "Listing only a single candidate is allowed under the rules, and it shows a very good aptitude for numbers. This is a math club after all."

"I demand a revote!" Kenny said. "We'll do the same thing and I'll win in a landslide."

"I'm sorry, there are no do-overs in elections," said Mr. Cosgrove. "The election stands, and Catherine is the new president."

"Then I quit!" Kenny said.

The Election Calculation

He rose, grabbed his backpack, and stomped to the door, followed closely by Buzz. Everyone else remained in their seats.

"Well?" Kenny asked, looking over the classroom defiantly. Everyone seemed to take a sudden interest in the tops of their desks, no one daring to meet Kenny's eyes.

"Fine! You can have your stupid club then!" Kenny said as he threw open the door.

"Wait!" Catherine said, stopping Kenny in his tracks.

"What do you want, cheater?" Kenny sneered.

"I just wanted you to know that I'll be picking the teams for the tournaments by choosing the best players, not just my friends. From what I've seen, you're really good at math. I'd hate for the team to lose you just because you're not the president anymore."

Kenny stared at Catherine in disbelief.

"C'mon, Kenny, let's go," Buzz said, tugging on his friend's arm.

"Hold on just a minute," Kenny said. "Maybe she's right. You and I are the best players on the team. They can't afford to lose us."

"But ..."

"It can't hurt to hang around for a few meetings anyway," Kenny said.

He returned to his seat and dropped his backpack to the ground. Buzz watched in amazement, then also returned to his chair. Kenny looked over at Catherine and said, "You're in charge. What do we do now?"

Catherine rose from her seat. "Now we do some math," she said.

Across the room, Trudy nodded. Catherine acknowledged her with a subtle nod of her own.

After math club was over, the Math Kids lingered behind.

"I have a few questions about the trick you pulled getting Catherine elected president," Jordan said.

"It wasn't a trick," Justin said. "It was math. I got the idea from that pink rose in the painting at Stephanie's house."

The Election Calculation

"What's a rose have to do with elections, or math for that matter?" Catherine asked.

"Well, the painting had all kinds of different flowers, but only one pink rose. The math club had more than one candidate, but only one Catherine. I figured if we could split the votes among candidates, but all of us voted just for Catherine, it would make her stand out, just like the pink rose in that garden."

"It worked, but I think we got lucky," Stephanie said. "If Trudy had voted for Kenny as her top candidate, he would have won."

"Actually, it would have been a tie if Trudy had Kenny first and Catherine second," Justin said.

"And then what would have happened?" Jordan asked.

"I was hoping Mr. Cosgrove would cast the deciding vote," Justin said. "With Kenny being such a jerk all the time, I thought he might pick Catherine."

"And what if he had decided to just flip a coin or something?"

"I was prepared for that," Justin said.

He reached into his backpack and pulled out a coin.

"You never know when you're going to need to have a coin flip go in your favor," he said. He turned the coin over to show it was heads on both sides.

"You wouldn't!" Stephanie said in disbelief.

"Nah, I guess not," Justin said, "but after everything

Kenny and Buzz did to me, I have to admit I thought about it."

"But isn't it better to know Catherine won fair and square?" Jordan asked.

Justin shrugged his shoulders and smiled. "What can I say? The numbers don't lie."

The End

Appendix

Checking to See if a Number Is Divisible by 3

To determine if a number is divisible by 3, simply add all the individual digits. If the sum of the digits is divisible by 3, then the original number is divisible by 3.

Let's check to see if 654 is divisible by 3:
6 + 5 + 4 = 15   Since 15 is divisible by 3, so is 654.

Let's check 527:
5 + 2 + 7 = 14   Since 14 is not divisible by 3, neither is 527.

Checking to See if a Number Is Divisible by 5

This is one of the easier division checks. If a number is divisible by 5, it will always end in either 0 or 5.

655 and 870 are both divisible by 5.
527 and 113 are not divisible by 5.

Checking to See if a Number Is Divisible by 11

It's easy to see that numbers like 22, 33, or 44 are divisible by 11, but what about numbers like 2,654?

Here's an easy check: Alternately subtract and add the individual digits from left to right. If that number is divisible by 11, the original number is also divisible by 11.

Let's check to see if 8,654 is divisible by 11:

$8 - 6 + 5 - 4 = 3$ Since 3 is not divisible by 11, neither is 8,654.

Let's check 5,291:

$5 - 2 + 9 - 1 = 11$ Since 11 is divisible by 11, so is 5,291.

Grappling Hook

A grappling hook is a device that usually has three or four metal hooks attached to a rope. The grappling hook is thrown onto an object, where at least one of the hooks can catch hold. The rope could then be climbed or pulled to retrieve the object. Grappling hooks were invented thousands of years ago and originally used to catch in the rigging of a ship to allow the ship to be boarded. They were also used during the D-Day landing in World War II to help soldiers climb the cliffs at Normandy Beach.

The Election Calculation

Grappling hooks are still used today. Army combat engineers can launch grappling hooks from a special rifle and then drag them to detonate mines connected to a tripwire. They are also used to repair communication cables running under the ocean. The grappling hook is dragged by a ship until it catches on a cable.

In the story, Justin didn't have much luck with his grappling hook, but maybe it was a sign that they shouldn't be used for trespassing anyway.

A Cool Foam Experiment with Hydrogen Peroxide

In the book, Justin used hydrogen peroxide and manganese dioxide to produce steam. Here is another cool experiment you can do with hydrogen peroxide. This is best to do outside as it can be a little messy.

Ingredients:
- 2 tablespoons warm water
- 1 teaspoon yeast
- Food coloring
- ½ cup hydrogen peroxide
- Dish soap
- Two-liter plastic bottle

Step 1 — Mix two tablespoons of warm water and one teaspoon of yeast in a cup. Stir until the yeast is completely dissolved in the water.

Step 2 — Pour ½ cup hydrogen peroxide into the empty bottle.

Step 3 — Add a few drops of food coloring into the bottle.

Step 4 — Squirt a little of the dish soap into the bottle.

Step 5 — Pour the mixture of water and yeast into the bottle. Stand back and watch colored foam pour out of the bottle!

Voting Math

People have worked for hundreds of years to come up with the fairest way of voting in elections; that's why Jordan was able to find so many voting methods.

Since Justin knew they couldn't beat Kenny in a traditional election, he found a way to get around the system by using something called bullet voting. Since Borda Count voting assigns points based on how the votes ranked the candidates, the system encourages minority voters (like the Math Kids in this book) to vote for just one candidate. That allowed Catherine to get a lot more second-place votes than Kenny, and her total score was enough for her to become the new president of the math club.

Thomas Edison

Thomas Edison spent years working to create a light bulb. He failed time and time again because the bulb would quickly burn out. When it was said that he failed, stories say he replied, "I have not failed. I've just found 10,000 ways that won't work." He tried thousands of materials before he finally found that a carbonized bamboo filament (the part of the bulb that glows brightly) would allow him to create a long-lasting bulb.

Solving math problems can sometimes take a long time, and we often must try different methods before we come up with a solution. We should not consider it a failure to find ways that don't work. Each "failure" helps us to learn and eventually succeed. Stick with it!

Coming Next!

The Missing Cache
*Book 11 in **The Math Kids** Series*

by
David Cole

Chapter 1

Catherine Duchesne took several tentative steps off the leaf-covered trail, staring intently at her phone. She frowned and then returned to the path that carved its way through the forest of yellow-poplar and pine trees. She took another few paces along the well-worn trail and glanced again at her phone. Convinced she was heading in the right direction, she continued walking.

"It shouldn't be much farther now," she said out loud, although there was no one to hear her. She was alone in the woods on a sunny Saturday morning, the cool air hinting at the arrival of autumn. It was still warm enough for shorts, but she was wearing a light jacket over her t-shirt. She stopped to take a sip from her water bottle, then slid it back into the side pocket of her backpack. She checked her phone one more time.

Catherine was on a treasure hunt of a sort, but this one was very different from the one that had taken her and her friends deep below the old Maynard mansion several years earlier. That search had been for real treasure. This time she was participating in an activity called geocaching, locating hidden objects using global positioning satellite, or GPS, signals. She had learned about geocaching at the club fair at the beginning of the school year. All the students at her middle school were encouraged to join two different clubs. She and her best friends all loved math, so joining the math club was an easy first choice. Picking a second club had proven to be much tougher. She had narrowed it down to robotics, photography, or geocaching. She had finally chosen geocaching because she felt a little sorry for Benny Dodson, an enthusiastic seventh grader who was the only other person in the club. Catherine was a little skeptical at first, but it had only taken finding her first geocache to get her hooked on her new hobby.

Geocaching used satellite signals to pinpoint hidden caches placed by other geocachers. While it could be done with a GPS locator, Catherine was using a geocaching application on her phone to lead her to the cache. The phone app could get her within about twenty-five feet of the hidden treasure, but then it was up to her to find it. On her first trip, she had found a waterproof box tucked in between the roots of a large tree. On another, she'd discovered a plastic container taped to the back of a wooden fence. Her last cache had been a small magnetic box stuck to the bottom of a metal bench.

Inside each cache, there was a log where you could

The Missing Cache

write your name and the date to prove you had found it. But sometimes there were also small items called swag. Benny had explained that swag was an acronym for "stuff we all get." The idea was to take one of the objects, usually small toys or pins or keychains, out of the cache and then replace it with something you brought. Catherine had put her art skills to work and come prepared with a homemade friendship bracelet to put into the cache. But first she had to find it!

Thirty minutes later, she was still searching. Catherine checked her phone for the fourth time to confirm she was looking in the right spot. The geocaching app said she was close.

"Close doesn't cut it," she grumbled. "It has to be here somewhere."

She used her foot to move a pile of leaves to one side. Nothing there. She was out of places to look. Frustrated, she sat down with her back against a tree trunk and pulled an energy bar out of her pack. Her good friend Jordan always said "there's no problem that a snack can't help you solve." Catherine wasn't sure if that was true, but she was hungry so she might as well eat something while she figured out where to look next. She tossed her backback on top of a moss-covered rock. She was expecting a dull thud, but the pack landed with a hollow-sounding plunk.

Catherine raised her eyebrows. She walked over to the rock and knelt down to examine it. She gave it a rap with her knuckles. She hadn't misheard. The rock sounded hollow. She smiled.

"Very clever," she said.

She lifted the *rock*. It was much lighter than a stone of that size should be. She turned it over. As she suspected, it was a plastic container shaped and painted to resemble a rock. The fake moss was a nice touch to complete the camouflage. She found a small clasp and opened the container. She had found the geocache! It was full of swag—small cars, a dozen plastic soldiers, two keychains, and several finger puppets. She dropped her friendship bracelet into the box and selected a hand-painted keychain.

She signed the logbook, carefully printing her name and the date. She looked through the last page of entries in the log. She saw that some people entered their name, while others put their geocache username. Catherine smiled at some of the clever names, including CacheMaster, GeoNinja, and TreasureTracker. She noticed the last person to find the cache had been here just a week ago. They had signed the logbook with "govson" and had included an email address. Catherine jotted the information down in a small notebook she kept in her backback. She planned to email the person to see how long it took them to discover the fake rock hiding place.

Before leaving, Catherine carefully placed the fake rock exactly where she had found it. She used a large leaf to

The Missing Cache

brush away her footprints. She didn't want to make it too easy for the next person searching for this cache. When everything looked like it had before, she slipped on her backback and headed back down the trail.

"Mission accomplished!" Catherine said. Whoever had hidden that cache had done a good job and Catherine was proud she had found it.

When she got home, she hung her backback on a hook in the mudroom. She took off her hiking boots before entering the kitchen.

"Hey, Dad!" she called out.

There was no answer. Even though it was a weekend, her dad was probably at the college, where he taught math classes, or at the offices of G-Knot, the company he had founded with her friend Justin's dad. Catherine powered up her laptop and logged into her email account. After entering the email address she found in the logbook, she wrote a quick message to the person who had found the cache the previous weekend.

Hi, govson!

I found the same cache you found last week on the Heritage Trail. How long did it take you to figure out it was a fake rock? I've only been geocaching for the past month, but this is my favorite hiding place so far. How about you?

I left a homemade friendship bracelet in the cache and took a painted keychain. Seemed like a pretty good trade.

What did you put into the cache?

Catherine

Catherine clicked send and signed off. Glancing at the clock, she saw she had another hour before her best friend Stephanie would be home from soccer practice. She decided to spend the time working on the packet of problems from the math club. The regional competition would be here before she knew it. As president of the club, Catherine got the final say on who would represent the two teams that Tyler Middle School would be sending to the competition, and she wanted to be well prepared. She was up against some really good math folks, and those were just the ones in her own club. There would be even more at the regionals.

Catherine was deep into a probability problem when she heard the screech of tires outside her house. She dropped her pencil on the coffee table and rushed to the living room window. Outside, a black car had pulled to the curb in front of her house. The car had a pulsating red and blue light in the rear window. As Catherine watched, a burly man in a black suit emerged from the front passenger seat. He walked quickly across the lawn, followed closely by the driver of the car. Catherine smiled when she recognized the driver. It was FBI Special Agent Carlson. Catherine's smile faded when she saw the tense expression on Carlson's face. Something was wrong!

She ran to the door and threw it open.

"What is it?" she cried out. "Is it my dad?"

"No, no," Agent Carlson said as he stepped onto the front porch. "This has nothing to do with your dad."

"Are you sure?"

"Absolutely," Carlson reassured her.

"Then what is it?" Catherine asked. "What's wrong?"

"It was the email you sent to govson," Carlson said.

"What about it?"

"Do you know who you sent it to?" the agent asked her.

"Not really," Catherine said. "It was just another geocacher. I found a cache today and they had found the same one last week."

Agent Carlson looked confused.

"Geocaching is like treasure hunting," she explained. "People hide containers, and you use GPS to find them."

"And you're sure you don't know this other geocacher?" the agent pressed.

"No, just someone named govson," Catherine said.

"That *someone* is Matthew Roberts," Carlson said.

Catherine's eyes widened as she recognized the name.

"Govson," she said. "Now that name makes sense."

Carlson nodded. "Yes, he's the governor's son."

"Am I in trouble for sending him an email? I was just asking him about the cache I found today," Catherine said. A puzzled look came across her face. "And how did you even know I emailed him?"

"No, you're not in trouble," Carlson said. "And the reason we knew about it is because we're tracking all attempts to contact Matthew."

"Why?" Catherine asked.

"Because he's been missing for three days," the agent said somberly, "and the governor suspects he might have been kidnapped."

Acknowledgments

As I finish this book, math competition season is coming up. This year I'm coaching at three different elementary schools. There are about fifty kids per team, so about a hundred and fifty kids in total! It's a lot, and hopefully I'm not biting off more than I can chew, but helping to coach these teams is one of my favorite things to do every year. As I was thinking about my part in the process—teaching math and strategy for the game of Equations—I'm always reminded of everybody else who is involved. There are teachers spending their own time to promote the competition, set up the teams, get money collected, sign teams up for the tournament, and arrange for bus transportation. There are the kids who participate, the parents who make extra trips to pick up their children after school, the other coaches, the team that runs the tournaments … the list goes on and on. The point is that none of this happens without support from a lot of people. It's those people who allow me to concentrate on the math, which is the fun part.

Writing The Math Kids books isn't much different. The books don't make it from my laptop to print and digital copies without the wonderful team at Common Deer Press. Amanda Lee and Caroline Fernandez do a great job of getting books to the right place and getting readers to notice them once they are there. Emily Stewart is an amazing editor who makes the books so much better than what I send her. Her attention to detail is only surpassed by her great story ideas. Shannon O'Toole designs beautiful covers and interior artwork. She's been a part of The Math Kids from the beginning and only gets better with each book. Kirsten Marion is there from beginning to end and I truly appreciate her faith and the direction she provides. These are the people who allow me to concentrate on writing books, which is the fun part.

Support on the home front is also second to none. My three kids, Stephanie, Jordan, and Justin (do those names sound familiar, Math Kids readers?) continue to be my inspiration. My wife Debbie fully supports my "writing hobby," even as it takes up more and more of my time with the addition of the *Emily and Sam* series.

And, of course, none of this happens without the readers. Thanks for continuing to follow the adventures of Stephanie, Jordan, Justin, and Catherine. I always love to hear from you. You can reach out to me through the math kids website (TheMathKids.com). Teachers and librarians —I'm always open for classroom and library visits. It's

The Election Calculation

one of my favorite parts of being a writer. Parents with younger kids, I heard your requests: my new series, Emily and Sam, is written for first and second graders. I hope your kids enjoy it as much as The Math Kids.

About the Author

David Cole has always been passionate about math. His background is in math, mechanical engineering, and computer science, and he has done everything from designing missile guidance systems to teaching college computer science classes to designing data center management software. He has coached many different math teams, and he ran a summer math camp for elementary school students for a number of years. He found that one of the best ways to teach math was to do it through games and stories. Most campers were reluctant to give up a week of their summer to math, but after attending once, they kept coming back year after year. The Math Kids series was born from the stories David told to get kids to understand and actually like math. David is the author of the eight previous books in The Math Kids series and is currently working on the next one. To keep up with the adventures of Stephanie, Justin, Jordan, and Catherine as they use their math skills to solve mysteries, deal with classroom bullies, and help their friends, check out TheMathKids.com.